Flora and Gretta Gauld
in Taiwanese dress

Jean Little

His Banner Over Me

VIKING

VIKING
Published by the Penguin Group
Penguin Books Canada Ltd, 10 Alcorn Avenue, Toronto,
Ontario, Canada M4V 3B2
Penguin Books Ltd, 27 Wrights Lane, London W8 5TZ, England
Viking Penguin, a division of Penguin Books USA Inc., 375
Hudson Street, New York, New York 10014, U.S.A.
Penguin Books Australia Ltd, Ringwood, Victoria, Australia
Penguin Books (NZ) Ltd, 182–190 Wairau Road, Auckland 10,
New Zealand

Penguin Books Ltd, Registered Offices: Harmondsworth,
Middlesex, England

First published 1995
10 9 8 7 6 5 4 3 2 1

Printed and bound in Canada on acid free paper ⊛

Canadian Cataloguing in Publication Data

Little, Jean, 1932–
        His banner over me

ISBN 0-670-85664-9

I. Title.

PS8523.I77E5 1995   jC813'.54   C95-930036-8
PZ7.L5Hi 1995

This book is for you, Mother.
Thank you for letting me tell it
even if I did get so much wrong.

He brought me to the banqueting house,
and his banner over me was love.

Song of Solomon 2:4

Author's Note

◈

This book is a novel based, sometimes very loosely, on stories I heard of my mother's childhood and youth. I wanted to tell it because I personally find it deeply moving but also because I suspect children today have no notion what it would be like to be separated from your parents for years at a time and have no way of communicating with them except by letters which travelled by ship. I also wanted to put on record the cost to missionaries' children of the call to "go into all the world and spread the gospel," though I never heard one of the "Gauld children" complain.

I lived with my grandmother for the last twenty-five years of her life, with my great-aunt Jen for the last thirteen years of hers, with Mother's sister Gretta for the last twenty-four of hers and with Mother herself for most of sixty years. I heard them all talk at length about their lives. I knew and talked with Uncle Harvey, Aunt Dorothy and their cousins John and David Balfour. I have let my brother Jamie and my cousin Ailsa read the manuscript and acted on their advice. My sister Pat has been with me and advised me countless times through most of its writing. We also have read carefully and lovingly diaries kept by Mother during the year she lived with her family in Toronto and started attending medical school.

In spite of all this, and in spite of what research I was able to do, many blanks remained in my knowledge and I had to invent whole scenes. All the most important ones did take place, however, in some way or another and all the significant relationships are as close to the truth as I could get them. I have "adjusted" facts, invented people, and joined bits and pieces sometimes to make a coherent story.

I used names that were close to real ones but changed any I thought would be hurtful to living people. I wish I knew more about Mother's years in Regina. I do know that, when I was close to fifty and asked her what was the proudest moment of her life, she said, "Catching Uncle Jack's fly ball and putting him out at Regina Beach the summer I was twelve."

Mother died after I'd written the first five chapters. As she read them, she would say, "Well, that's not what really happened, of course, but you are telling a good story." Then she would correct a detail or two where I had gone too far astray. She died at age eighty-nine on July 12, 1991 after a hard fight with cancer. I miss her sorely. Finishing this book kept her closer to me a little longer.

I hope she would still say, "Well, you have it wrong. But you've turned it into a good story."

Jean Little
November 1994

Table of Contents

1
Hoy Bit

◈

Jesus loves me, this I know,
For the Bible tells me so;
Little ones to him belong,
They are weak but He is strong.
Yes, Jesus loves me!
Yes, Jesus loves me!
Yes, Jesus loves me!
The Bible tells me so.
Anna Bartlett Warner

"Foreign devils!"

Gorrie Gauld was sitting on the garden wall with her older sister, Gretta, when she heard the angry words. Both girls turned sharply to see who had shouted them. Gorrie was used to being called a "foreign devil." There were so few white people in Tamsui that she and her family attracted friendly attention wherever they went. Many Taiwanese not only stared at her and called her a "foreign devil" but commented freely on her fair skin, her greenish eyes, her big feet and her long brown hair.

1

"They have no idea you speak their language, Flora, or they wouldn't say such things," Mother had told her. "Think how startled you'd be if you'd seen only Chinese people all your life and then, all of a sudden, you saw us."

By now, Gorrie almost enjoyed listening to the comments. But this was different. She spotted the man at once. He was riding by in a rickshaw. Although he had shouted in Chinese, he wore a Japanese soldier's uniform. And he was glaring at Gretta and her as though they were invading cockroaches.

"Gretta, why is he staring at us that way?" Gorrie asked.

"Don't point. It's rude," Gretta said automatically.

"He's staring *and* he's calling us names. That's much ruder. What does 'foreign' mean exactly?"

Gretta did not answer. She had scrambled to her feet on top of the wide wall. She towered over her sister and the rude man. Gorrie, peering up at her, saw her dark eyes were blazing with righteous wrath.

"*Gai-jin!*" Gretta yelled in Japanese.

To Gorrie's delight, the man quailed slightly and looked away. Then he shouted at the rickshaw man to go faster. Gretta stayed on her feet until he was out of sight. Then she sat down again and, a little breathless, replied to Gorrie's question.

"Foreigners are outsiders. That's what '*gai-jin*' means too. Outside person. What cheek to call us foreigners when he's one himself!"

"We can't be foreigners. We were born here," Gorrie protested, shocked at the very idea of being thought an "outsider" in the place she had lived all her life.

"Yes, but Father and Mother weren't born here and we aren't Chinese. We don't really belong, but we're not half as foreign as that Japanese."

A small boy was riding by now, perched high on the back of a plodding water buffalo. He grinned at them and crossed his eyes. Gorrie laughed, crossed hers in response and felt better. Four men trotted past carrying a sedan chair. A baby with a bare bottom scampered by in the opposite direction with his giggling big sister in hot pursuit.

Finally, across the road, Gretta's friend Mei-lin opened the gate in the wall of her family's home to admit a coolie carrying baskets piled high with vegetables. This was what Gretta had been waiting for, a glimpse of her friend. She waved wildly. Mei-lin waved in return but went back inside.

"I can't be a foreigner," Gorrie said, ignoring her sister's sigh as the gate closed. "I have a Chinese name."

Gretta, longing to go over to her friend's house but forbidden by Father to leave their own garden, was sulking and pretended not to hear what her sister had said. Gorrie waited for her to calm down. Then she spoke in a light, teasing voice.

"I get called by three names."

"What do you mean? I'm the one with three," Gretta retorted as Gorrie had known she would.

"I'm Gretta Lilias Victoria. You're only Flora Millicent."

"Don't call me Millicent," Gorrie growled. "I mean names people use. Mother and Father call me Flora. You and William call me Gorrie. And Ah Soong calls me Hoy Bit."

"Hoy Bit doesn't suit you. Flower Honey. It sounds far too sweet. Mine is better. Ah-gyek means Precious Jade and green is my favourite colour. Oh, look. There's Mei-lin on the roof now, helping her auntie."

Again Gretta waved but Mei-lin's aunt was scolding away at her, and, once the laundry was hung on the roof poles to dry, Mei-lin went back inside without even looking in their direction.

"I'm sick and tired of sitting here," Gretta said, swivelling around so that her back was to the tempting street.

"Let's play Joseph and his brothers," Gorrie suggested at once. She had wanted to all along but had waited for her sister to be in the right mood. "You can be Joseph and have the coat of many colours."

Gretta groaned. She was fed up with Gorrie's games. You had to be Daniel in the lion's den one minute and Cinderella the next. They also played they were shipwrecked or in boarding school or running a hospital or conducting a church service. All of them, even three-year-old William, loved to preach.

Gretta opened her mouth to say "No!" and then made the mistake of looking into Gorrie's pleading eyes.

"Oh, all right. Where's William?"

Their parents insisted the three of them stay together out of doors. The girls were to keep an eye on William. He had run away once. The whole house had been in an uproar until Ah Soong, the amah, had found him down the road chewing sugar cane with his friend Kim Buun.

"He's right over there on the grass watching ants," Gorrie said, pointing. She swung her legs back over the wall and slid to the ground.

"Will, you're going to be Joseph's brothers," she called to him.

"No," William said in a muffled voice. "Go away. Leave me alone."

Gretta and Gorrie gaped at him. Will was famous for his happy-go-lucky nature. He never whined, rarely lost his temper and almost always went along with Gorrie's games.

"What's wrong, William?" Gretta asked. "Don't grizzle. Tell us."

"My throat hurts," he whimpered. "I want Mother."

Gretta jumped off the wall and advanced on him. "Sit up and let me see," she commanded. "I'm going to be a nurse."

William clamped his lips tight shut and shook his head. Gretta sighed and ran for help. Gorrie heard the "Hungarian Rhapsody" break off.

"What is it now?" she heard Mother ask, sounding annoyed.

A moment later, Margaret Ann Gauld swept out

the back door with Gretta trotting behind. The
minute she felt William's burning face and peered
into his throat, she changed from a busy, confident
music teacher to a very anxious mother. She lifted
William up, big as he was, and started for the house.

Then Ah Soong ran out and tried to take him
from her.

"No, no, Gau Bok Sun Yu," she said. "Think of
baby."

Mother darted a sidewise look at her daughters
and shook her head slightly at their nursemaid. The
girls took in both the words and the significant
glance. They kept their faces blank, hoping to learn
more.

"I'm all right," Mother said. "But William's ill.
Send someone to find Gau Bok Su and tell him
we'll need Dr. Tanaka."

Ah Soong scurried off. Mother, clutching
William, followed.

"Stay outside," she called back to the girls. "We
don't want you catching this, whatever it is."

Her daughters watched her go and then
exchanged glances.

"I think she's going to have a baby," Gretta said
softly. "I heard them talking in the kitchen."

Mother "having a baby" made no sense to
Gorrie.

"We can't play Joseph without William," she
said in a dejected voice.

Gretta had forgotten their plan. She was confused for a moment. Then she laughed.

"I could read *Black Beauty* to you instead," she offered.

"Goody, goody!" Gorrie said, clapping her hands and forgetting both William and Joseph. She and Gretta settled into the big wicker chairs on the cool verandah and began at the beginning of the book.

Neither of the sisters was familiar with flesh-and-blood horses. In Taiwan, loads too heavy for coolies were carried by water buffalo or oxen. Yet Mother and Father often spoke of horses they had had in Canada. Mother especially missed these legendary creatures and loved to tell of the day she had ridden her brother's new horse, Lar, in a race against two of his friends.

"My parents would never have let me ride him," she always said. "But he'd been broken by a woman and was not used to carrying a man. I talked to him and held him back until I saw the finish line. Then I loosed the reins and said, "Go it, Lar!" The others weren't expecting me to catch up, let alone fly past. When we raced by and won, my brother cheered."

She had been sixteen that day, but she still told the story so vividly that the children felt they had seen the race with their own eyes. No wonder their copy of *Black Beauty* had loose pages and a worn binding. They almost knew it by heart.

The girls stayed outside all afternoon, feeling worried and abandoned. At suppertime, Ah Soong gave them their bread and milk in the kitchen.

Jean Little

"How's William?" Gretta demanded.

The amah avoided her searching eyes.

"He's asleep. Open your mouth, Hoy Bit," she said, spooning the food into Gorrie as though she were a baby. "The doctor is coming back when your father is home. William be all right soon. What is that you say, Ah-gyek? Dorry hunky?"

The sisters giggled as she had meant them to.

"You know it's 'hunky dorry'," Gretta said. "You're teasing."

Ah Soong's warm smile comforted them. They went to bed without a fuss but they were still wide awake when they heard voices in the hall. With one accord, they ducked under the mosquito netting that was draped over their bed and crept to the door.

"It's scarlet fever, I'm afraid," Dr. Tanaka was saying. "But he may have a mild case. You'll have to isolate him. Can you manage that?"

"Of course. How long before we know if he's going to be all right?"

Mother's voice was husky. The girls huddled closer and went on listening.

"We'll know in less than a week whether it's a mild case."

"My cousin had it," Father rumbled. "It left her with a bad heart."

"Yes, it can lead to complications. But with careful nursing, we may prevent that," the doctor said. "Lots of fluid, lots of rest..."

His gentle voice died away down the hall.

Gorrie and Gretta sprinted silently across the

bamboo mat and scrambled back into bed. Yet getting to sleep was hard.

"Are you going to be a missionary when you grow up?" Gorrie asked, not wanting her sister to drift off and leave her to worry alone.

The older girl shook her head so hard that the pillow bounced.

"No," she said. "I'm going to nurse sick children."

"Missionaries can nurse sick children," Gorrie pointed out.

"I know. But missionaries have to tell people about God and Jesus. I hate talking about things like that."

"Don't you think Jesus loves us?"

"Of course. But it's private. I can't talk about it. I'm never going to be a missionary. Never, never, never."

"Sing to me," Gorrie said. Mother usually did this, if she was free, but they had not seen her since she had taken William into the house.

Gretta began to sing "Jesus Loves Me." The familiar words lulled Gorrie. Yet, when she was almost asleep, her sister's voice broke off abruptly.

"What's wrong?" Gorrie said sleepily. "Why did you stop?"

Then she heard, inside her head, the words Gretta had just sung.

> Jesus loves me, He will stay
> Close beside me all the way;

If I love Him, when I die,
He will take me home on high.

Gorrie sat bolt upright and stared at her sister.

"William won't die, will he?" she asked, a quaver in her voice.

"Of course he won't," her sister snapped.

"Jean died," Gorrie whispered.

"I know," Gretta said, "but William won't. Go to sleep."

Gorrie had not been born yet when their sister, Beatrice Jean, had died of pneumonia. It had happened during the Gaulds' last furlough in Canada. Jean had been not quite two years old. Gretta had been just three but she said she remembered her. Gorrie had seen photographs of her, a small, big-eyed solemn child clutching a doll. Mother never spoke of her without tears.

Gorrie did remember clearly the cook's two sons who had died of typhoid fever a year before. And she knew of other children's deaths...

But William was so alive.

Gretta began to hum "Sweet and Low." Gorrie, feeling lost and frightened, dove into the safety of sleep.

Ah Soong was there when she opened her eyes. She helped Gorrie into her clothes and combed both girls' long hair. Mother did not come to say good-morning and was not in her place at the breakfast table. Their father looked unusually solemn. Gorrie was alarmed.

Gretta burst out, "Where's Mother? Is William all right?"

"William is a sick little chap," their father told her. "Your mother is going to be busy caring for him for a few days. Ah Soong and I will look after you two."

He sounded helpless. He could preach sermons and draw plans for buildings and run prayer meetings and make things out of wood but he had never taken care of them. The thought of Father combing their hair or helping them dress struck Gorrie as so comical she almost exploded into laughter.

"I'm going up to see William," she announced.

Her father caught hold of her and drew her back.

"No, Flora. Both of you are to stay away from your brother. Scarlet fever is contagious. William needs quiet."

"Can't we even play?" Gorrie asked uncertainly.

"Of course. But play down here and in the garden. Now let's say a prayer together for your brother."

The girls knelt and bowed their foreheads against his tall black knees. His hand rested on Gorrie's hair as he began to pray. "Bless Thy children, Gretta and Flora, and send Thy healing to William, if it be Thy will. We ask this in Jesus' name, Amen."

It was time to eat. Yet their father had not asked God to bless the food. It was strange, too, to be eating breakfast without their mother and Will. While Gorrie watched Father's big hands peeling an orange for her, she tried to imagine scarlet fever. She knew what "scarlet" meant. The Mounties in faraway Canada wore scarlet coats. Her father had shown her a picture. If William was bright red, she wanted to see.

All day, she could not get near him. But just before supper, when the doctor came again, her parents left William to speak with him and Gorrie seized her chance. Ducking under the smelly sheet that hung over his door, she whisked across the room to her brother's bed. She pushed aside the mosquito net and peered at the William's face.

He was not scarlet at all. He did look hot. His cheeks were flushed. But nowhere near scarlet. Then she glimpsed the bright red rash that covered his neck and what she could see of his chest. So that was the scarlet part.

"Mother," he croaked, looking straight through Gorrie as though she were invisible, "Mother, my throat hurts me."

"It's me, Gorrie," Gorrie whispered.

William stared up at the ceiling with wide frightened eyes.

"Make the snakes go away," he whimpered.

It was dim in the bedroom but Gorrie knew there were no snakes. He was seeing things. His sister almost fled. Yet she could not leave him like this. She reached out and softly touched his forehead. It was burning hot.

"You're safe in bed, William. There aren't any snakes here," she soothed him. She felt grown-up

and important until William twisted away and
began to cry in a thin wail.

Gorrie heard, with a grateful heart, the flip-flap-
ping sound of Ah Soong's shoes in the hall. She ran
to her.

"Ah Soong, he doesn't know me," she cried.

"Oh, Hoy Bit, you shouldn't be here," her amah
scolded gently. "Run downstairs before your mother
sees."

Gorrie wakened the following morning with a terribly sore throat. Surely she hadn't caught William's
germs in her fleeting visit to his room! She winced
at the thought of what Father would say when he
found out. Well, she wouldn't tell. Ah Soong
wouldn't tell either.

At breakfast, Gretta complained about not being
allowed to go outside the garden. Gorrie let the
familiar argument wash over her unheard.

"We must keep you safe," her father said
patiently. "There are Japanese soldiers everywhere.
Men in an army of occupation are bored and restless. I don't think they would harm a child but I
don't want trouble. Until things settle, you must
stay in our own garden. Do you understand,
Gretta?"

"Yes, but I'm nine," Gretta muttered. "I can run
away from soldiers."

Gorrie thought about the soldier who had called
them "foreign devils" and wondered if he had been
bored and restless.

Her parents had Japanese friends. Dr. Tanaka and his wife were among them. Mrs. Tanaka had given Gorrie a small Japanese doll in a pretty flowered kimono, which she dearly loved. Her parents trusted Dr. Tanaka to care for the whole family.

So that Japanese soldier who had called them "foreign devils" was not rude because he was Japanese but just because he was a rude man.

"Is William better?" she asked without looking up.

Their father stared down at his untasted porridge.

"The doctor says he'll be better if...when his fever breaks."

He got up suddenly and strode out of the dining room.

"He didn't pray or say 'Excuse me,'" Gorrie marvelled.

"He couldn't. He was crying," Gretta said. "I'm not hungry."

They sat and eyed each other uneasily. They weren't allowed to leave the table until they had finished their food and been excused. But neither of them had any appetite left. And nobody was there to excuse them.

Ah Soong came in and looked at their half-full bowls.

"Wait," she said.

A moment later, she was back with two bowls of savoury Chinese food. The smell of meat dumplings brought back their hunger. Ah Soong smiled as their chopsticks flew. She was convinced that nobody should start the day eating oatmeal porridge.

An hour later, the girls were once more sitting side by side on the garden wall. Then, without warning, a group of five Japanese soldiers turned the corner and came swaggering toward them. Neither girl realized, at the time, that the men were drunk but both sensed something was wrong with them. Gorrie froze. Gretta, showing off for any of her Taiwanese friends who might be watching, stuck out her tongue.

Three of the five soldiers burst into loud laughter. It was too loud. The shortest one got very red and shouted at the others in staccato Japanese. The fattest unslung his rifle and pointed it at the sisters.

Gretta leaped off the wall, yanking Gorrie after her. The soldiers roared with even louder laughter and came running. Letting go of Gorrie, Gretta dashed for the safety of the house.

"Run, Gorrie," she screamed over her shoulder. "RUN!"

Gorrie wanted to. But she had landed off-balance and crashed to the ground with one arm twisted beneath her. Usually she would have lain still and howled. Not now. Sobbing, she struggled to her feet and tore after her older sister. But Gretta had longer legs and she ran like the wind. In a blind panic, Gorrie tripped over a gnarled root and shot headfirst into an iron-hard tree trunk. She sat down with a jolt that jarred her teeth and stared dizzily after Gretta.

The soldiers were going to get her. She knew, without turning her head, that they were all jumping over the wall right now and racing toward her. But she could not move.

Her desolate cry stopped Gretta in her tracks. She dashed back.

"Gorrie, stop," she begged. "Father will hear. The men are gone."

Then Ah Soong arrived. Gretta began explaining. But their amah was holding Gorrie and looking at her with worried eyes. She put her hand on the child's forehead.

"Oh, Hoy Bit," she said in a small scared voice, "you have it too."

She picked the four-year-old up as though she were a doll and bore her into the house. Mother took one look and put her to bed in William's room.

By the time Dr. Tanaka came, Gorrie had the scarlet rash and was as delirious as William had been. She was not seeing snakes though. Gigantic menacing soldiers chased her through her nightmarish dreams.

"We'll have to cut her hair off," a faraway voice said.

Her mother cried. But even when they cropped her long brown hair short, Gorrie stayed lost in a fevered world. Several times in those first few days, the sick child glimpsed, through the mist, her mother's drawn face bent above her. Young and ill as she was, Gorrie longed to dispel the fear and anguish in Mother's eyes. She had caused this, she dimly remembered. She had done it by going into William's room.

"I'm sorry, Mother," she cried out in a small, cracked voice. "I won't go in again."

Only Ah Soong knew what she was talking about. She smoothed back the soft, dark stubble of hair on her Hoy Bit's head and kept her secret.

William recovered in ten days but Gorrie did not. She had pain in her head and back. She felt too weary to play. Her ankles grew puffy. William delighted in peeling bits of dead skin off his palms and the soles of his feet but Gorrie couldn't be bothered. Even when Mrs. Tanaka brought her a miniature garden in a big soup bowl, Gorrie gazed at its tiny humped bridge over a little river with mossy banks and its trees made of twigs without reaching out her hand to touch them. It seemed magical but remote and unreal.

"I'm afraid she has nephritis—inflammation of the kidneys," Dr. Tanaka said. "Bedrest is the only treatment. Lots of fluids, no salt. But chiefly rest."

Gorrie did not protest. She did not care. She didn't feel like playing anyway. She lay limply and watched leaf shadows flickering across the high ceiling and waited for the world to right itself.

"Poor little plucked chicken," Father said, resting his big hand on her shorn head.

At last, after what seemed like months, she was well enough to be carried downstairs. She lay on the sofa, listlessly turning the pages of one of their fairy-tale books.

"Come on out," William called to her, as he ran through the house chasing Ah Soong's nephew.

"Maybe you should get some fresh air, Flora," her mother said. "Ah Soong will carry you. You can sit on the lawn for a few minutes and watch the clouds and get a little sunshine."

Gorrie knew she was strong enough to walk but she let Mother call to Ah Soong.

"Coming in one jiffy," Ah Soong called from outside.

Waiting, Gorrie gazed at her mother, who had been so busy, always doing two or three things at once. She usually laughed a lot and told funny stories and played jokes on people. Why was she so quiet now? Was she just tired? Or was she sad about something? She even moved more slowly...

"Mother," Gorrie asked, fear sharpening her voice, "are you sick?"

Mother looked at her and smiled a little.

"No," she said gently. "Just a bit tired."

Then Ah Soong arrived, her hands wet from doing laundry.

"I think Flora needs some fresh air," her mother said. "Could you take her outside? She can sit on the verandah or right out on the grass perhaps."

Ah Soong lifted Gorrie easily. She set her down on the grass, half in the shade but next to where she was spreading white things to dry and bleach in the hot sun. She went back to work and Gorrie looked at the bright sky, the big trees and the scarlet poinsettias in the hedge. Next to her was a row of

Father's white dog collars, the ones that let everyone know he was a pastor. They looked funny sitting lined up, stiff and round, without a neck inside them.

Something hissed.

She turned and sat paralyzed. A cobra had reared its deadly head up from inside a stiff collar and was poised, ready to strike the moment she so much as blinked.

Gorrie never forgot those long, taut seconds while she and the snake stared into each other's eyes. She did not see Ah Soong's eyes widen in horror or glimpse her waving frantically to the gardener to come. She did not hear him running barefoot across the grass.

Wham! His hoe sliced down, cutting off the cobra's head before it could strike. The snake's blood splashed onto her, staining the hem of her skirt.

Then the scream which had been choking her split the air.

"No, no, Hoy Bit." Her amah snatched her up and ran with her toward the safety of the house. As she did, she poured a stream of Chinese words into Gorrie's ear. But the child hardly heard. She cried in great wrenching sobs all the way back to the living-room sofa.

Then Mother's arms were around her and Ah Soong was rushing away for some hot sweet tea. Gorrie's teeth clattered against the rim of the cup when she brought it. Mother held her so tightly it hurt and kissed her tufty hair.

"Poor baby," she kept saying. "My poor baby."

Finally Gorrie pulled away a little.

"I'm not a baby," she said gruffly. "I'm almost five."

Twenty minutes later, Gretta ran in with letters the mailman had entrusted to her.

"Letters from home," she sang out, waving them. "One from Gord, one from Harvey and one from Aunt Jen."

Mother took them and went to the table for her ivory letter opener. As she began to slit the envelopes open, Gorrie saw her hands were still shaking. Had Gretta noticed? She glanced at her sister. Gretta was looking not at Mother but at her.

"Ah Soong told me about the snake," she said. "But you look fine. I have to go. Mei-lin has come to play in our garden."

She dashed away. Mother laughed.

"Are you really fine, Flora?" she asked.

Gorrie cuddled down into the quilt Ah Soong had wrapped around her and sipped the sweet tea. She no longer felt her heart hammering inside her chest. She began to feel proud of her narrow escape. Almost getting struck by a cobra was like something in a book.

"Yes," she said cheerfully, "but I nearly died, didn't I?"

Mother nodded slightly and began reading Gordon's letter aloud to her.

Darling Mother,
> How are Lily and Milly and Willy?
> Harvey has a cold but Aunt Jen is not
> worried. I had a cold two weeks ago
> and I had a fever of 104. Don't worry
> though. I am all better and, by the time
> you get this, Harvey will be fine too…

Without warning, tears began streaming down Mother's face.

Gorrie threw off the quilt and ran to her. She patted her mother's back and yelled for help. Father came. He put his arm around his wife's heaving shoulders and leaned down to kiss her wet cheek.

"What is it, my dear?" he asked. "Tell me. We can set it right, with God's help. Is it the baby coming?"

They seemed to have forgotten she was there. Gorrie wanted to run to tell her sister that she had guessed right but she stayed where she was.

"It's…it's everything," her mother gulped. She told in snatches about the snake. Then she went on, still half-crying, "The boys are growing up without us. Jen is goodness itself but they're my boys. And Gordon says he had a cold and his fever went up to 104. That's too high for a fifteen-year-old, Will. Harvey had a cold when they wrote. Gordon could have gotten pneumonia and died without our even knowing."

"He's all right now?" Father interrupted to ask.

"Yes, he's all right. He wrote the letter. But Flora isn't getting well as fast as she should. And Mother and Father... Well, it isn't fair for all their care to fall on the others. I know God needs you to be here, Will, and I said I'd be yours for better or worse. I don't want to leave you alone here. But I've been away from home for fifteen years with only one trip back. When we did go on furlough, the months flew by. We had so many people to see and so many speeches to make... I need to be with the boys and Father and Mother and just live there with them all for awhile. I'd come back, Will..."

There was a long silence. Then Gorrie's father spoke very gently.

"Next spring," he said. "The baby will be old enough to travel then. But Flora is better, Gret. Just look at her."

"I am," Gorrie put in, speaking for herself. "I'm as better as anything."

It must have been the right thing to say, for her mother gave a shaky laugh and her father beamed at her.

"Good," he said. "Now, little pitcher with the big ears, you run and tell your sister and brother and Ah Soong and the cook and anybody else you can find that, in a few months, you're going home to Canada. You'll be crossing the ocean. William will like that."

A trip to Canada! Gorrie could not believe it. She had never in her life had such exciting news to tell.

"Gretta," she shrieked, tearing out the door. "Gretta, Will, we're going home to Canada."

"Canada," William shouted from halfway up the

stairs. "What's Canada?"

"You goose," Gorrie scolded, delighted to find him so ignorant. "It's a place, a big city like Tai-pei, with a big school for boys and things. It's across the ocean. Ocean is another word for river."

Behind her, her parents laughed aloud. And Gorrie discovered, with that reassuring sound, that she really was well. Well enough to want to run to find Gretta and tell her the other amazing news. A new baby was going to Canada with them.

2
Mixed Blessings

◈

...God be with you till we meet again.
Keep love's banner floating o'er you.
Smite death's threatening wave before you.
God be with you till we meet again.

Jeremiah Rankin

It was time to go. Gorrie, eager for the journey to begin, jigged up and down impatiently. For weeks she had been saying goodbye to everyone over and over again. She had been kissed so much she thought her face must be nearly worn off. She had stood still and smiled while her picture was taken dozens of times. Once, she and Gretta had been dressed up in Chinese clothes for a photograph. She had not smiled that time. She had felt like someone else. Hoy Bit instead of Gorrie maybe. It was Ah Soong's favourite picture of them.

"Come back soon, Hoy Bit," her amah said now, hugging her yet again.

"I will," Gorrie promised, wiggling free. She did

not like being clutched by anyone, even this woman who had looked after her since the day she was born. "Don't worry. Father's work is here. We'll be back."

Ah Soong turned away quickly. She guessed that when it was time for the Gaulds to return, her Hoy Bit would be left behind to go to school in Canada.

Gordon, the oldest of the Gauld children, had lived in Taiwan until he was six. Then his parents had gone on furlough taking with them Gordon; his three-year-old brother, Harvey; Gretta, a toddler; and their new baby, Jean. They returned, a year later, with only Gretta after Jean died of pneumonia. Harvey, then four, had been left to keep Gordon company. Both boys had stayed in Canada with their loving aunt and uncle but it still seemed monstrous to Ah Soong.

And now Gretta had turned ten, and Gorrie five, and William was almost four.

Ah Soong had become a devout Christian but, if the Lord God himself came down from heaven and commanded her to send her children away, she knew she would not do it. It wasn't natural.

"I'll go on board with you, Gret, and help you get settled," Father said at that moment. "Come on, youngsters."

"Come *on*, Gretta!" William pulled hard on his sister's hand, desperate to run up the waiting gangplank.

Mother sniffed and, carrying the baby, began to move through the throng. Gorrie had her hands full. She had been entrusted with a string bag crammed with food. Each of the children had also been allowed to take whatever toy she or he could carry. Gretta had taken a battered rag doll which had been given to her on her first birthday.

"They'd throw her away if I didn't," she said defensively.

Gorrie had, in her spare hand, three books, *Black Beauty*, *Little Lord Fauntleroy* and *Grimm's Fairy Tales*.

"Why books when you can't even read?" her sister asked.

"You can read them to me," Gorrie said, not meeting her eyes.

She could read lots of words now but she had kept her knowledge secret. If she told, she was afraid her parents and Gretta would stop reading aloud to her.

Holding tightly to both the bag and the precious books, she pushed her way through the crowd, struggling not to lose sight of her relations.

Suddenly everyone who had come to see them off began to sing "God Be with You Till We Meet Again." Gorrie heard the sound of those loving voices with a sudden lump in her throat but she did not really listen to the words until they sang the third verse.

> God be with you till we meet again.
> Keep love's banner floating o'er you.
> Smite death's threatening wave before you.
> God be with you till we meet again…

She pushed away the unsettling image of "death's threatening wave" but she really liked the line "Keep love's banner floating o'er you." She knew about that banner. She had asked her father once what the words meant and he had shown her the verse in the Bible. "He brought me to the banqueting house, and his banner over me was love." It was like a bright flag streaming in the wind above them, a flag which reminded them and others too that God cared for them and they belonged to Him.

"*Peng-an*," their Taiwanese friends began calling out.

"*Peng-an*," Gorrie shouted back from her place deep in the forest of legs and bundles.

That word, meaning "peace," was the greeting exchanged by Christians in Taiwan. It was like the banner. It said something special about them.

After the long wait, they suddenly began to board the ship. The gangplank bounced under their boots and made a clanking noise as they crossed it. Gorrie wanted to run to the safety of the far side but she was caught in a stream of people slowly boarding the vessel that would take them on the first part of their journey. She pushed closer to her mother's long skirt instead. Then they were on the wooden deck. Even though it moved slightly, it felt wonderfully solid after the gangplank.

Gorrie ended up half-smothered by the press of grown-up bodies. People around her wept and laughed and called farewell messages. Handkerchiefs were waved.

"Gorrie, look!" William yelled.

She tried to push through the wall of bodies but nobody shifted. Finally her father, making for the gangplank to leave the ship, saw her problem and lifted her up and over the crowd, setting her down next to her brother. He kissed the top of her head and leapt for the temporary bridge between ship and shore. He just made it across before it was pulled up.

Then the children held their breath as the water began to widen and Father was left standing on the pier, looking like a bulky giant among the mob of shorter, slighter Taiwanese. Coloured streamers were thrown from those on the ship to those gathered on shore. They stretched out, rainbow ribbons, connecting them for a few seconds longer to the loved ones left behind. But one by one, they broke or were pulled out of clutching hands. Gorrie turned her head away for an instant, not wanting to see the vivid strips of pure colour falling into the sea and becoming sodden rubbish. Then she looked back, needing to keep Father with her until the last moment.

The land actually seemed, to her, to be pulling away from them. With a last mournful hoot of the ship's horn, they were off. And the ocean was not just a river. It was bigger than she could ever have imagined. It had no edge.

"Flora, William," Mother called.

"We're here," Gorrie called back. But her voice was lost in the slap and wash of waves, the thrumming of the engine and the hubbub made by the throng of passengers. She could not turn and go to her mother anyway. She was glued to the ship's rail, watching, watching her father shrinking to a speck and then disappearing as the ship turned out to sea.

Gretta thrust her way through and fetched them then. The Gaulds went clattering down the steep companionway and crowded into their small stateroom.

"Where do we sleep?" William asked, staring at the two narrow berths.

"You'll be with me. Baby Dorothy can sleep in her basket. Your father fixed it so it won't slide. Gorrie and Gretta will have to share the top bunk. It'll be a real adventure," their mother said, doing her best to sound excited about the cramped quarters.

Gorrie did not have to pretend. Excitement bubbled up in her; she wanted to dance. Then she saw Mother had tears in her eyes. She must be missing Father.

Gorrie was trying to think of something comforting to say when the ship lurched and the floor under their feet slanted and rolled slightly. Mother's look of sadness changed to a strained expression her children had never before seen. Gorrie tried to place that look but couldn't. Then Dorothy began to cry. She must be hungry or wet. And Ah Soong wasn't here.

"I'll change her," Gretta offered, seeing Mother catching hold of a chair which was fixed to the floor.

"If only I were a better sailor," their mother moaned.

She sank onto the chair and watched Gretta lift the baby into the bottom berth and change her diaper. Gorrie and William watched too, impressed by their sister's competence but not about to let her guess it. Then Mother took the baby and nursed her. The children were slightly abashed since their mother usually fed Dorothy in her bedroom. But they had all seen Taiwanese mothers breast-feeding their babies in church and on trains. They smiled as Dorothy sucked greedily, making little piggy grunts of pleasure.

Once the baby was settled in her basket, though, Margaret Ann Gauld crawled into the bottom bunk. She lay with her eyes closed.

"What does she mean? Mothers aren't sailors," Gorrie asked her sister.

"She gets seasick," Gretta muttered. "Father told me to look after her. And Ah Soong taught me how to take care of Dorothy. But I think..."

The ship rolled again. Gretta did not finish the sentence.

"Can we go exploring?" William asked.

"Go. By all means. But don't be a nuisance," their mother murmured, as though she were far away somewhere.

By the time the younger two came back, Gorrie felt slightly queasy herself. Gretta had unpacked some fruit and biscuits for their supper.

"We'll go to the dining room tomorrow," she

said. Then, glancing at Mother who had turned her
back to the food, "or the day after."

"I'm hungry now," William said. He ate three
biscuits, a chunk of cheese, a banana and an orange.
Gorrie found she did not want much. She nibbled
one biscuit and stopped.

That night, the wind came up and the sea grew
rough. As the ship began to pitch about, Mother
grabbed a basin and vomited. Instantly, both Gretta
and Gorrie brought up their boots too. William was
disgusted.

"I don't feel a bit sick," he bragged. "Not one bit."

If Gorrie had not been sure she was dying, she
would have punched him. To everyone's relief, the
baby slept peacefully.

Gorrie was the first to get her sea legs. On the
second day, she found she was suddenly as cheer-
ful as William and ravenously hungry. The two of
them ate their way through all the provisions in the
cabin. Then, in the nick of time, Gretta recovered
enough to take them to the big dining room. It was
wonderful sitting there, with huge linen napkins
draped over their fronts, being waited upon by a
steward. They had never dined in such splendour
before—and to do it without an adult reminding
them of their manners every other minute was bliss.

After that, for a day or two, Gretta stayed in the
cabin to act as nurse while Gorrie and a jubilant
William raced about the ship, exploring every passage, opening doors wherever they could, getting
chased out of the engine room. Finally they knew

their way around the whole ship and relaxed. Mother became more or less herself. The baby, who had a runny nose, was fretful but not seriously ill.

One blustery day, nobody but Gorrie even wanted to go up on deck. She galloped up and down, pretending she was Black Beauty running free with his mother in the meadow. When she was out of breath, she held onto the ship's rail and swung her body idly back and forth.

She yearned to try "skinning the cat" as she had seen some older boys doing. But if Gretta saw her turning upside down and showing her drawers she would run hotfoot to tattle. Mother might just laugh and tell Gretta not to be such a goody-goody. You never knew with Mother.

She was twisting around to check on her big sister's whereabouts when she heard words that made her stiffen to attention.

"I just went by Mrs. Gauld's cabin," an amused voice was saying, "and there she sat, still pale green from being seasick, hard at work on a pile of mending, with the little boy playing beside her and that sickly baby in a basket at her feet, and she was singing, 'Count Your Blessings.' Can you believe it?"

It was Mrs. Mulholland. Her husky laugh was unmistakable. At the sound, Gorrie jerked, as though someone had thrown a sharp pebble and hit her squarely between the shoulder-blades. She did not swing around to stare at the gossiping adults. Her hands clenched into white-knuckled fists and her cheeks burned. How dared they laugh at her mother? If only her big sister had been by her side, she knew Gretta would have sprung like a tiger to their mother's defence. She would have marched right over and shouted out scalding words which would have made them ashamed of themselves.

Picturing this, Gorrie flinched. Maybe it was better that Gretta had been somewhere else.

"What blessings has the poor woman got to count," Mrs. Mulholland went on, "with her husband on the other side of the world and all those children to care for by herself? If I were in her shoes..."

"Hush, Milly," a man's low voice warned. "I think that little girl over by the rail is one of hers."

"Oh dear, I didn't mean...," Gorrie heard the lady murmur, sounding really sorry.

"Let's go below. You have to be careful. Her children are all over the ship."

Gorrie waited until they had gone. Then she dashed, pell-mell, down the companion-way and burst into the small crowded cabin.

There sat her mother, just as Mrs. Mulholland had said. Dorothy, so fretful the past day or so, was asleep at last in her basket. William was trying to build a tower with the alphabet blocks Father had made for him before they left Taiwan. Agitated as she was, Gorrie paused for an instant to watch. It was almost impossible to build a block tower with the motion of the ship working against him but William kept trying. As she stood poised, the ship

lurched and this tower, too, came tumbling down.
William sighed.

Gretta was scrunched up in the berth reading
Little Lord Fauntleroy again. And Mother was darning one of Gretta's stockings. She did *not* look one
bit green—but she did look white and tired. Of
course, she was singing. Gorrie's mother always
sang while she worked. Especially when she was
doing a job she detested.

> When upon life's billows
> you are tempest tossed
> And you are discouraged,
> thinking all is lost,
> Count your many blessings.
> Name them as they fly.
> And you will be singing
> as the days go by.

Gorrie leaned against the arm of the chair and
stared down at the heel of the long black stocking
pulled tight over the darning egg in her mother's
left hand.

"Mother, don't sing that," she pleaded softly.

Mother shot her an astonished glance. Then her
eyes narrowed. She went on darning but her needle
moved more slowly.

"Why ever not?"

Gorrie bit her thumbnail. She remained silent. If
she told, Mother would not like it. Yet Gorrie must
stop her mother's singing somehow. If she could

even get her to hum instead…

Gorrie sighed. Mother would never hum when she could sing. Everybody on the ship must have heard her by now. Maybe they were all poking fun at her behind her back.

Mother's long darning needle stopped filling in the hole. She turned in her chair and looked searchingly at her small daughter's averted face. She had stopped smiling. She reached out automatically and pulled Gorrie's hand away from her mouth.

"Cat got your tongue, young lady?" she demanded. "I asked you why I was to stop singing. Tell me why now, please."

"I heard a lady talking," Gorrie mumbled. "She said you hadn't any blessings to count. She said Father was on the other side of the world and your baby was sick and you had too many children and…and no blessings."

Gretta came out of the bunk like a small volcano erupting. Hair on end, face red as fire, she stood with her hands on her hips and glared at her younger sister.

"Well, of all the cheek!" she blazed. "Who dared to say such a thing? I wish I'd been there. I'd have given them a piece of my mind."

"Be still, Gretta," Mother's voice had an edge that hushed even her oldest daughter. "And don't interrupt."

Gorrie felt heartened as Gretta flounced over and plunked her bottom down on the lower berth. It was not often Gretta Lilias Victoria said the wrong thing. Gorrie turned back to smile at her mother. But Mother did not return that smile. Her cheeks, so white a moment before, had also grown flushed. Her eyes, usually merry, sometimes impatient, were now bright with anger. Gorrie stared, hoping it was just anger that made them sparkle that way. Not tears. She couldn't really be seeing her mother's eyes shine because of tears...

Then, to Gorrie's intense relief, Margaret Ann Gauld threw back her head and laughed. The listening children gaped at her, reassured by that laughter and yet disturbed by it too. There was something not quite right about its sound. Seeing their uncertainty, she laughed again, more naturally, and gave Gorrie's shoulder a quick pat. Then, gazing deeply into their worried eyes, she spoke slowly, making sure they heard each tender word.

"I have so many blessings. That lady did not understand. Each one of you is a great blessing. And Father too, of course. We know how dearly he loves us. And God's love is our greatest blessing of all. You know that, don't you?"

The three of them nodded solemnly. Even Gorrie, who sometimes felt God expected too much, knew His love was a blessing.

"And we have a loving family in Canada waiting to welcome us," her mother went on, "and remember all our kind friends in Taiwan. I am a very fortunate woman with almost too many blessings to count. Come on. You sing with me. We'll show the world how blessed we are."

Gretta began to sing immediately. William hummed along. Gorrie winced inside as her mother's and sister's strong, clear voices rang out, sending their defiant message sounding through the open door to anyone with ears to hear. The baby's eyes flew open but she did not cry.

Mother, still singing, scooped her up and wrapped her in her woolly shawl. She rose and started for the door. Clearly, the Gauld family was going on deck.

"Sing, Gorrie," Gretta hissed, giving her a poke in the back.

William laughed and began chanting a slightly mixed-up version.

> Count your blessings, Gorrie. Sing,
> Gorrie, sing.
> Count your blessings, baby. Sing, sing,
> sing.

Gorrie wished they would all hush up. Yet she was proud of them too. Singing that way was like thumbing their noses at all the ladies who made fun of their family. And she was part of that family. She fell in behind the singers now marching out the door.

We're like a parade, she thought. All we need is a flag.

Then she remembered the singing at the pier and smiled. They did have a flag even if nobody could see it. His banner over them was love. With hardly a wince, Gorrie Gauld opened her mouth and joined in the chorus. And once she did, she didn't sing softly; she sang at the top of her voice.

3
Family Reunion

Blest be the tie that binds
Our hearts in Christian love.
The fellowship of kindred minds
Is like to that above.

John Fawcett

"Move over, Gretta. Let William sit by the window. Wave goodbye to your grandmother, all of you," Mother said as she settled herself, their bags, the baby and the three older children into their train seats.

"I'm waving to my auntie," William said firmly.

Margaret Ann Gauld opened her mouth to scold him and then shut it without speaking. After all, they would not be seeing her battle-axe of a mother-in-law for several weeks, and besides Mother Gauld should not have called William "a thrawn laddie with the manners of a booby."

Gorrie waved obediently to the two women on the London station platform. Aunt Nell beamed at her and waved back but Grandma Gauld's hands, gloved in black cotton, gripped the handle of her large, black purse as though she expected someone to snatch it away from her any minute. Her small wrinkled face, sunk in the shade of her black bonnet, did not relax its nutcracker expression for one instant.

"Do you think Grandma Gauld sang Father lullabies and rocked him when he was a baby?" Gorrie asked her mother.

Mother laughed.

"Aunt Nell was twelve when your father was born. Perhaps *she* did the singing," she said. "She has always seemed a happy woman in spite of being the only girl. Watch for Seaforth, children. We mustn't miss our station."

Gorrie sat and thought about the two days she and her family had spent at the Gaulds' after the long train trip from Vancouver. They had all managed to sleep, crammed into the little cottage by the Thames River. Father's brother, Uncle George, and his wife, Aunt Jen, had come to dinner. Gorrie had liked Aunt Jen Gauld. But it was muddling having two Aunt Jens, one on each side of the family. Gretta had everyone straight but Gorrie and William had endless trouble.

"Can we go to see Buckingham Palace?" William had asked upon being told Grandma Gauld lived in London beside the Thames.

"We're in Canada, William," Gretta had said quickly, hoping Grandma Gauld had not heard him. "This is London, Ontario."

Gorrie, seeing his downcast expression, knew how he felt. The only thing she loved about Grandma Gauld's was sitting in the little rocking chair which had belonged to Aunt Nell when she was a child. Even though he was younger, William was already too big for it. Gorrie had felt almost mean leaving it behind in a house where no one else could fit into it.

Gorrie hoped Mother's mother was not like Father's.

In the whole time they had spent with the old lady, her granddaughter had not caught her smiling once. Yet Grandma Gauld had cracked a couple of dry little jokes and had even laughed twice. Her laugh had sounded more like a bark. Two other things made this grandmother different from anyone else the Gauld children knew. First came the white cap she wore all day. William believed that she had no hair on top and wore it to hide her bald head but Gorrie and Gretta were positive he was wrong.

The other fascinating but unsettling thing was her broad Scots speech. It had been unnerving to have her fix her beady black eyes on you and say something you only half understood. At breakfast, she had stared at Gorrie and said, "Yon Flora is a peaked wee bairn, I mun say. Ye mun gie her some oatcakes wi' a slather of heather honey or she'll nae mak auld bones."

Whatever "auld bones" were, Gorrie had no wish to make them.

"We haven't far to go this time," Mother said, looking at their tired faces and then staring out the window, searching for familiar landmarks.

Gorrie was glad the travelling was about to end. She was sick and tired of stopping to visit complete strangers and watching her mother kiss and hug them as though they were her nearest and dearest. Although Gorrie was frightened of meeting the many people Mother had told them would be in Kippen, she wanted to get there and sleep in a bed that stayed still and would be hers for more than one night.

"Will Gretta and I have to sleep together in Kippen?" she asked.

"Yes. There'll be quite a houseful, especially at first," Mother said.

Gorrie did not really mind. She was sure the bed would be wide enough for comfort. She had always slept with her sister.

The train shuddered to a stop in the little town of Hensall, waited for less than three minutes and started up again with a whoosh of steam and a long mournful toot of its whistle.

"We'll be pulling into the Kippen station in a minute," Mother cried, breaking in on her daughter's thoughts. "Get ready, William. Gretta, is my hat on straight? Don't hang back this time, Flora. They're your relatives. You mustn't be bashful. Your big brothers are there and all the rest are your own flesh and blood too."

Gretta and William had their noses flattened

against the dusty window. Small as she was, Dorothy seemed to be straining to see out beyond them. She leaned forward and waved her pudgy hands at everything in sight. Gorrie stood up and backed into the aisle. Past their heads, she saw the small station slide into view and, on the platform, what looked like hundreds of people.

Mother leaned over Gretta and William, shouting excited greetings and comments even though every word was drowned out by the hiss of steam.

Gorrie felt her stomach knot with nervousness. If only Father were here! He was so big and strong and quiet that he would have given her courage. He was shy too. Putting her small hand into his large one and feeling it give hers an understanding squeeze would have made all the difference.

The train shuddered to a stop. Mother handed Gorrie the smaller grip and the string bag with the oranges. For this last leg of the journey, the three books Gorrie had chosen to bring along had been packed in Mother's big trunk.

"Let *me* take Dorothy," Gretta was insisting, struggling to wrest her little sister out of Mother's grasp. But her mother did not let go.

"No, Gretta. You might drop her," she said unfairly. "Get hold of William's hand and take the carpet-bag. Now lead the way. Flora, you go next. No. I'm coming last to make sure we've got everything."

Gorrie, feeling braver with things to carry, pushed her way between the scratchy green seats.

She could tell by the set of Gretta's shoulders that her big sister was furious. Gorrie didn't blame her. Gretta would never have dropped Dorothy. Mother herself had said hundreds of times how dependable her darling Gretta was.

Gorrie understood, all at once, that her sister was mad as hops not because she really believed Mother thought her clumsy but because she guessed that Mother simply wanted to show off their beautiful baby herself. After all, not one of the people waiting out there had ever laid eyes on Dorothy.

They had not seen William either. Or Gorrie, come to that. She wasn't little and winsome, like Dorothy, but William, with his dark hair coming down to his eyebrows and his big brown eyes, was. Gretta must have realized that too. She reached back and grabbed his sticky hand.

"Let *go!*" he roared, doing his best to jerk free.

Gorrie grinned. He hadn't a chance. Gretta Lilias Victoria had him in an iron grip and she was looking incredibly smug. Poor Will.

"You can't be baby Gretta! You *are!* But you're so grown up. The last time we saw you…"

"And who's this big fellow? Young William. Why, he's the spitting image of Dave when he was little."

Gorrie gulped and took Gretta's place on the high steps. She stared down, hoping against hope she would escape notice.

"This one must be Flora, the flower of the family."

The teasing voice had to belong to her big brother Gordon.

Gorrie concentrated on getting herself and the bags down the steep steps. Then her chin shot up. She glared at her tall brother. The laughing fifteen-year-old boy looked just like his picture only much more alive. Harvey, three years younger, stood next to Gord. Harvey was not laughing. Two smaller boys, who must be cousins, burst into giggles. "Dandelion or Primrose?" Gordon kept going, egged on by their shrieks of delight.

"My name is Gorrie. Only grown-ups say Flora."

"Gorrie's a nice name," said Harvey as he took the suitcases. "Cut it out, Gord. She's just four."

"I'm five," she flashed at him. "I've been five for ages."

The three months since her birthday did feel like ages. She stared at Gordon. Although his eyes were still filled with laughter, they were looking over her head. As Mother appeared, his face lit up with joy. "Mother," he cried out, and leapt up the two steps to sweep her into a bear hug which Dorothy shared.

"Oh, my son, how tall you've grown," Mother said shakily. "I'll look at you properly in a moment. Lend a hand. Lend two."

Then she gave him the heavy valise she had been pushing along with one knee.

Gordon bore it away as though it weighed a feather.

Gorrie was not fooled by her mother's light tone. She stared up into Margaret Ann Gauld's shining eyes. The last time Mother had seen Gordon, he had been just seven. Gorrie felt a tightness in her throat.

Harvey, next to her, cleared his. Maybe he could not even remember Mother. He'd been four when they had left him in Canada to keep Gord company. Why wasn't he stepping forward like Gordon?

Gorrie, so shy herself, guessed why. All the staring eyes were concentrated on her mother and baby sister. He wanted Mother's and his first meeting after so long to be private. Maybe Mother did too. Even though she was not a bit shy herself, she had not come over to hug him.

"This is the new baby! What a little love!"

Gorrie and Harvey stood side by side, watching all the strangers kissing her mother and leaning down to chuck William under the chin and hug Gretta.

Dorothy shrieked, all at once, and held out her arms to her Aunt Jen. And, in that instant, while everyone's attention was diverted, Mother and Harvey exchanged a quiet, loving look nobody but Gorrie caught.

Good, she thought.

Then Flora Gauld, eyeing the mob of excited people, discovered that she recognized almost every face. She'd seen photographs of all of them in the fat albums Mother and Father had at home in Tamsui. But the flesh-and-blood people were so loud, so tall, so active and so overwhelming. There was only one who looked as nervous as Gorrie felt and that was a little girl hiding behind Uncle Henry's leg and sucking her thumb.

Gorrie clung to the bag of oranges with both

hands so she need not hug anyone back. Every so often, she was squeezed and released, cooed over and set aside. She waited stoically for it to be over. All at once, it was. They were trooping out to the two waiting carriages.

"The big boys can walk," Aunt Jen was saying. "Dave and John can jump in the back and squeeze William in between them. I'll keep Gret and the baby up front with me. The girls can go with you and Mime, Henry."

"Gretta and Flora, this is your cousin Jean," Uncle Henry said, putting his hand on the small girl's head. "She's a bit rowdy so don't copy her bad ways."

"Henry, you're as bad as Gordon," Aunt Jemima said, getting into the second carriage.

"Up you go, Jeanie," Uncle Henry chuckled, swinging his small daughter up to sit on her mother's knee. Before helping Gretta and Gorrie into the carriage, he turned to Mother and said he was glad they'd arrived safe and sound. While he was making this speech, Gordon stepped up behind the girls and grabbed Gretta.

"Up you go, Grettie," he mimicked softly, hoisting her up onto the high seat. She landed with a thud and glared at him.

Gorrie hid a grin. Gretta loathed being called Grettie. Nobody was allowed to make fun of her precious name. How had Gordon guessed? He'd better not call her Millicent or she'd get back at him somehow.

Not wanting to be grabbed like her sister, Gorrie slipped around the carriage and scrambled in beside Aunt Mime without help. She felt smug for a moment. Then she felt abandoned as she watched her mother getting into the other carriage, chattering a mile a minute to Aunt Jen, not even glancing over to see how her daughters were faring. The smaller boys, her cousins Dave and John Balfour, clambered in behind their mother, pulling William after them.

"Giddap, Betsy," Aunt Jen sang out, and off they went.

Uncle Henry untied the horse and swung in next to his wife. He smiled warmly at his nieces.

"I expect you're confused, meeting so many people all at once," he said. "I'm Uncle Henry Iveson and this is Aunt Mime, your mother's oldest sister. We have two older girls at home. And that little chatterbox on Aunt Mime's knee is your first cousin Jean."

Chatterbox! Did he mean the thumb-sucking child? Why, she had not spoken a single word yet. But then, neither have I, Gorrie realized suddenly.

"I'm Gretta," Gretta was introducing them primly. "And this is my sister Gorrie. Flora is her proper name. Can't Jean talk?"

"Oh, she never stops," Uncle Henry said solemnly. "Just like your sister. We're always begging her to give our ears a rest."

Jean, still sucking her thumb, gave a tiny snort of laughter. Gorrie could feel herself smiling a little too. She liked Uncle Henry.

"Welcome to Canada, both of you," Aunt Mime said softly.

"Keep an eye out," Uncle Henry went on. "We are now entering the outskirts of the great city of Kippen."

Gorrie gazed around expectantly. Mother was always telling them stories about Kippen. She and her sisters and brothers had all been born and brought up here. Grandpa had had a blacksmith shop here for years until he had lost his sight. Since then he and Grandma ran the Post Office and kept the General Store.

But where was the city? All she could see was a gravel road with a handful of houses lined up on each side of it. There were two churches and a shop. Tall bushes were in bloom and they crowded close to the houses with their purple and white flowers tossing in the breeze. A small tan-coloured dog ran out from a wide white house with a verandah. But that was all she saw. No city.

"Where…" she began to ask. But before she could put her question, Uncle Henry was telling his big horse to "Whoa."

The other carriage, having gotten a head start, was already drawn up to a hitching post in front of the wide white house. Mother was running up the steps and throwing her arms around an old lady who stood waiting there. Behind her, an elderly man with a long white beard was getting slowly to his feet. Gorrie stared at the couple. They must be Grandma and Grandpa Mellis. And even though she

was still in Uncle Henry's carriage, Gorrie could tell
they were all smiles. Not like Grandma Gauld at all.

Aunt Jen, with Dorothy in her arms, was now
following Mother up the walk. The boys were
already chasing each other around the chestnut tree
in front of the house. Aunt Mime got down from
the high seat and Gretta and Jean jumped to the
grass the minute she was out of their way. Gorrie,
who had been sitting behind her uncle, rose uncertainly, wishing again for Father. Her knees wobbled
and the palms of her hands grew damp. She hesitated, hoping her mother would turn and call to her to
come.

"Come on, girlie," said Uncle Henry in a deep
voice.

His arms, almost as good as Father's, lifted her
down.

The little dog, yipping excitedly, ran up, sniffed
at her skirt and tore away toward the house.

"That's Fleet," Aunt Mime said. "He's eight
years old now but he forgets his dignity when people come. He will remember your mother, I'm sure.
Gret spoiled him so when he was a pup."

Gorrie watched. The little dog certainly did
remember her mother. He leaped up at her, pawing
frantically at her skirt and barking hysterically until
she, brushing away tears, gathered him up into her
arms. Fleet immediately washed more tears off with
great sweeps of his enthusiastic tongue.

"Fleet, you fool dog, do you really remember
me?" Margaret Ann Gauld said huskily. "I've been

gone seven years."

Gretta stepped up and patted the dog's head. Gorrie saw Mother smile proudly at her.

"Mother, Father, here's my Gretta," she said, turning to the old couple. "I'd never have gotten this far without her help. But I can't wait to see the old place. Let's go in."

Only much later did Gorrie realize that her mother was as overwhelmed by everything as she was herself. Standing in the yard watching her vanish into the unfamiliar house with the dog still in her arms and with dependable old Gretta close behind her, Gorrie felt utterly forsaken. A great wave of longing for Ah Soong and Father rose in her. A river of tears threatened to pour down her face. In less than ten seconds, she knew she would burst into a babyish howl.

I won't, she thought fiercely, forcing the flood back with all her will. I won't cry.

She loathed making a spectacle of herself and, even more, she hated being fussed over and pitied.

"Grandpa, here comes Flora, the flower of the family," Dave shrieked at that instant. "She's very quiet because flowers can't talk, you know."

"I think she's a snapdragon," John shouted, trying to drown out his younger brother. "Or maybe a shrinking violet. She's small enough."

Gorrie was saved from crying by the hot rage which sprang up in her at their teasing. How dare these horrible boys make fun of her name! She hated them. She hated Canada. She hated Mother for hugging a dog and forgetting her. She was furious at Gretta, who was supposed to be her protector but had walked away without a backward glance. Most of all, she despised the boys, big and little, who had called her "the flower of the family"—as though she were not Gorrie any longer.

She longed to fly at them, biting, kicking and scratching. But she had promised not to bite. On the ship, she had bitten Mrs. Mulholland because the woman had kept saying she would steal their baby. Mother, scandalized, had given Gorrie a spanking and made her promise never to bite anybody again.

Biting would be risky anyway. The boys were too big. Even Dave, who was also five, was half a head taller than she. Whatever she did must be done from a safe distance—like David smiting Goliath.

That was it! She waited until nobody was watching. Then she bent down as though to tie her shoelaces and scooped up a few pebbles. Keeping them hidden in a fold of her skirt, she bided her time. Then, when everyone was watching Grandpa taking the baby from Aunt Jen, Gorrie let fly.

The first pebble missed. Nobody noticed it landing in a flower bed. The second small stone hit Dave's ear.

"Ow!" he yelped, clapping his hand to his head.

"What's the matter now?" his mother asked.

Gorrie flung her third missile. It struck John squarely on the back of the neck. As he jumped and yelled, "Ouch!" Gorrie's fury was spent. She dropped the last two pebbles. But William had seen.

"She did it," he said gleefully, pointing straight at his sister.

"What did you do that for?" Dave demanded, rounding on her, his face reddening.

"Don't you call me Flora," Gorrie ground out from between gritted teeth, her wrath rekindling. "Don't ever call me 'the flower of the family' again."

"She bites too," William put in, his eyes gleaming. "She bit a lady on the ship. Mother spanked her."

Harvey and Gordon came striding up just in time to hear the interchange. Gord threw back his head and laughed. Dave's and John's glares turned to sheepish grins.

"Would Spitfire suit you better?" Harvey suggested quietly, his eyes twinkling like William's.

"'Spitfire' would suit me just fine," his little sister said.

Then she dashed into the house to find her mother.

4
A Job Worth Doing

Work, for the night is coming!
Work through the morning hours;
Work while the dew is sparkling;
Work 'mid the springing flowers;
Work while the day grows brighter,
Under the glowing sun;
Work, for the night is coming
When man's work is done.

Anna Louisa Coghill

One Friday morning in June, Gorrie Gauld slid out the back door without being noticed. She stepped onto the grass and ran soundlessly until the big snowball bush was between her and the kitchen window. Then, safe from observation, she shut her eyes and lifted her face so that the warm sunlight and the gentle wind could wash over her cheeks and closed eyelids.

Both the sunshine and the summer breeze felt so different from the hot sun and steamy wind in Formosa, as her Canadian family called Taiwan. The flowers were different too. Gorrie decided to walk all the way around the big house and name all the blossoms she had never seen before she came to Canada. So short a time before, they had just been names to her; now she knew each flower's face and fragrance. Her chores could wait for once.

"Sweet William," she chanted softly, laughing a little at the name. "Petunias, pansies, bleeding heart, peonies, irises, lily of the valley…"

She stooped to pick one of the last remaining stems of lily of the valley and held the tiny sweet-smelling bell-like blooms up to her nose. No perfume you could buy was as lovely, she was sure. Most of the flowers smelled nice too but she loved lilies of the valley best.

The front door opened. Gorrie was about to duck back out of sight when she realized it was only Grandpa coming out to sit in the sun. He couldn't see her because of his blindness. She took a careful step backward. She was sure she had moved silently but she had forgotten Fleet. The little dog peered around the verandah post and wagged his tail furiously. Grandpa's head swung around.

"Who's there?" he demanded.

"It's me, Flora, Grandpa," she called back, her voice just loud enough to reach him. "I'm looking at all the flowers."

Fleet settled down at Grandpa's feet. He spent

most of the time watching over her grandfather. The old man stroked the dog's head and gave a quiet laugh.

"Keeping out of your grandmother's way, I'll wager," he chuckled. "'Satan finds work for idle hands.' That's what her mother told her and she's always remembered. Before I lost my eyesight, she used to try to keep me busy every minute of the day. She's a powerful woman, your grandmother."

Gorrie was not sure whether it was safe to agree with him. She had never before talked to him all on her own. You could not say whatever you liked with Gretta or Mother or Grandma listening and apt to butt in at any moment. Now she could say what she liked.

She stayed silent, thinking what to say. He sighed.

"Don't worry, child. Your secret is safe with Fleet and me," he said. "I'll even play something to cover any noise you make. A special song for your grandmother who practises what she preaches."

He picked up his concertina and started to play. Gorrie waited to see what he would choose. She did not recognize it until he began to sing.

"Work, for the night is coming
Work through the morning hours;
Work while the dew is sparkling;
Work 'mid the springing flowers…

She laughed and backed up.

"Ouch. Get off my toes!" her little brother yelped.

Gorrie turned to peer at him. Then she glanced back at their grandfather. Even with Fleet snoozing beside him, he looked lonely somehow. Before Aunt Jen had taken her boys and gone back to Regina, Dave had played an uproarious game with the old man. Dave would run around the table or duck under it and call, "You can't catch me, Grandpa. Try and find me."

Then Grandpa would lean over, his long snowy beard stretching down like an extra hand, and poke his cane under chairs and behind the table legs. Dave would shriek with laughter and dodge out of reach.

"David, you're too big to tease your grandfather like that," Grandma Mellis would say. But even Gorrie knew that she didn't mind Dave's play any more than Grandpa did.

"Why don't you hide on Grandpa, William?" she prompted softly now. She was not brave enough to do it herself. She was sure, anyway, that Mother and Grandma would not think it proper for a girl to rush about and tease the way her mischievous cousin had done. But William was a boy.

William stared at her and then shook his head very hard.

"Why not?" Gorrie insisted.

"I'm not Dave," William said. "I'm William."

"But..." his sister began to argue.

"I won't do it, Gorrie, and you can't make me," William sing-songed softly. Then he dashed away.

His sister watched him running down the long garden to the barn. She sighed. He was going out to
pet the horse, Betsy. If only she were a boy, she
could go too. Instead, she had to help Grandma do
the dusting and make the beds. She wished, not for
the first time, that they had brought Ah Soong to
Canada with them. She could have helped with the
housework and set Gorrie free. Never once had she
had to make a bed in Taiwan.

But Ah Soong was busy taking care of Father.

If only her grandmother wasn't so fussy.

"Fuss-budget," Gretta muttered when Grandma
made her straighten out the knives and forks and
spoons she had shoved any old which way onto the
table in the big kitchen where they ate.

Gorrie knew exactly how she felt. She had made
the beds with Grandma every morning since they
had arrived. During the week, Gordon and Harvey
boarded in Seaforth, where they went to high school.
While they were in town, she only had to help with
three beds—Mother's, the big one she and Gretta
shared and William's cot. Mother did Dorothy's little
trundle bed although Dorothy was always in bed
with Mother by morning. None of the children ever
set foot in Grandma and Grandpa's room downstairs but Gorrie was certain Grandma was every bit
as particular over making their big bed.

Grandma always took every blanket or quilt or
sheet off the bed one at a time, folded each carefully
and laid it over the back of a chair. Starting from
scratch, she then made the beds "properly."

I could do it in half the time all by myself if she'd only let me, Gorrie thought glumly. Then I could go play in the barn too.

Why not try it? Grandma was showing Myrtle, the hired girl, how to get stains out of William's clothes. Gretta was at school. Mother was making bread. If Gorrie slipped back in and ran, right this minute, she could have it all done by the time her grandmother was free to begin.

She was up the back stairs in a flash.

Yank. Twitch. Pull. Smooth. Plump up the pillow. Straighten out the coverlet. Gretta's and her bed was finished. Gorrie darted across the hall to the boys' room and sped to William's cot in the corner. Will had a straw mattress to sleep on. He was a restless sleeper. Every night, he tossed and kicked so that, by morning, everything had come untucked. But she could fix that in two shakes of a lamb's tail.

No time to shake the straw mattress until it looked fat and comfortable again. Never mind. William wouldn't care. Yank. Tuck under. Pull straight. Grab up the pillow. She was punching it to fluff up the feathers inside it when she heard Grandma's slow steps on the stairs. Gorrie plunked the pillow into its place and stood waiting. She could feel her heart start to drum against her ribs as those deliberate steps reached the bedroom door. What would Grandma say?

The old lady stood still for what seemed like a full fifteen minutes and studied William's small bed. She did not smile. She did not speak one word.

She just looked.

Gorrie, looking too, saw a suspicious lump down near the foot and noticed, for the first time, how the counterpane drooped down and touched the floor in one spot. The spot where William had lain was flattened. She moved over to stand in front of it and held her breath, braced for a scolding.

Grandma Mellis did not say a word. She went to the head of the bed and silently removed the coverlet. She folded it neatly and laid it over the back of the chair. Gorrie stared at her, still expecting a tongue-lashing. Grandma took the blanket off and began folding it.

She was not going to say a word. She was going to make the bed exactly the way she would have done if Gorrie had not tried to beat her to it.

Gorrie hurried over to help. She could feel her face burning. Even her ears felt hot. She banged the straw mattress up and down until dust flew, half-choking them both. Grandma Mellis sneezed but said nothing. Gorrie was furious at her but she knew, too, that Grandma liked things done her way.

The two of them moved across the hall. Gorrie marched over to the bed she and Gretta shared. She dragged off the top quilt and struggled to fold it neatly.

Grandma reached out, plucked it out of her hands, gave her two corners to hold and they folded it together. Then Gorrie, head down, took it to the chair.

"We'll turn the mattress," said Grandma.

It was heavy but they managed. Gorrie longed to run out of the room. Wasn't Grandma ever going to get the lecture over with? Would she tell Mother?

She wondered suddenly if Mother would have left the bed the way Gorrie had made it. She thought probably Mother would.

When they had finished Mother's bed too, Grandma looked at her granddaughter. Gorrie ducked her head again and stared hard at her bootcaps. Grandma's strong hand tilted her chin up instead.

"A job worth doing, Flora," said Grandma Mellis in her quiet but very firm voice, "is worth doing well."

When her grandmother turned away without another word and headed for the back stairs, Gorrie knew that was the end of it. But Flora Gauld also knew that she could have been reading *The Water-Babies* for ages if she had not had to take such time and trouble over that awful bedmaking. When she grew up, she would get the wrinkles out and that would be all. Then she would have hours left over for reading.

Head down, she followed Grandma along the hall. Then her head jerked up. She could not leave it like that. She shouldn't be thinking disobedient thoughts and pretending to be meek and mild. It wasn't honest. Besides, she ached to tell Grandma the truth about all housework.

"Grandma," she said softly to the disappearing back.

Grandma turned and waited. Gorrie cleared her throat and looked hard at the hem of her grandmother's skirt.

"It's neater, making beds that way," she muttered, "but it's a terrible waste of time. You could be reading or playing with...William."

She had been going to say "playing with Betsy" but the idea of her stately grandmother playing with a horse was too much even for her vivid imagination.

She glanced up into the old lady's calm face. Her knees quaked under her and she wished with all her heart that she had kept her thoughts to herself.

"Run along then," Grandma Mellis said without any change in expression. "William is waiting and Betsy is probably getting impatient for her carrot."

Gorrie fled. As she raced down the long garden walk, she wondered how Grandma could know about Betsy's carrot. Mother could read their minds but Gorrie had not known grandmothers had the same uncanny gift.

She gave Betsy her carrot and finally located William playing with the barn cat's newest kittens.

Later that morning she overheard her mother and grandmother talking. Gorrie was hiding from William behind the snowball bush right below the kitchen window.

All morning she had wondered what Grandma had said to Mother about her. She was sure her mother would be very angry indeed.

"Flora is a courageous child," Grandma said.

"What do you mean? Was she saucy to you or Father?" Mother asked, instantly guessing the truth.

Gorrie tensed as she waited for Grandma's answer.

"No, nothing of the kind. She has lovely manners and a good mind. She simply pointed out to me that, in her opinion, housework is a terrible waste of time. I didn't tell her I often agree with her."

The two women laughed.

"I remember reading in Jen's diary, 'Housework, housework, housework… I'm so sick of housework,'" Mother said. "I think she had been beating carpets."

"I dislike most the unending nature of it," her grandmother said slowly. "You just get a job finished when it is time to begin all over again. Sometimes, it seems to me that I clean up the same mess day after day after day."

"Mending," Mother moaned. But Gorrie caught the laugh in the moan.

"You might like it better if you practised it more often, daughter," Grandma said tartly. "Now you were wanting Aunt Janet's gingerbread recipe…"

Gorrie forgot all about William and the game they were playing. Grandma didn't like housework either. And Mother had laughed as though she too felt like taking a holiday. Was that the way all women felt? If so, why didn't they run away from it all sometimes?

She went around to the front of the house, thinking furiously about what she had overheard.

"Gorrie, you're It. It's my turn to hide."

"All right, William. Go and hide. Who's stopping you?"

"You are," William said. "You have to hide your eyes and count. All you do is sit there like a numbskull."

Gorrie closed her eyes, leaned her face against her crooked arm and began to count loudly. She'd keep going to three hundred. That would fix him.

Through her counting, she could hear Grandpa's concertina on the verandah above her playing again.

"Sixty-one, sixty-two, sixty-three..." she droned on, trying to recognize the tune. It was a dancy one and her counting speeded up in spite of herself.

Her grandfather sang:

> Daisy, Daisy, give me your answer, do,
> I'm half crazy over the love of you.
> It won't be a stylish marriage.
> I can't afford a carriage.
> But you'd...

Gorrie stopped counting to listen. Did Fleet like concertina music? He lay there, one paw on his nose, sound asleep. Gorrie began humming along, forgetting William. Then, in the middle of the song, Grandpa changed into another.

"Work for the night is coming," he sang.

Gorrie stared at him for a second and then realized, almost too late, that he was sending her a warning. The front door was opening. She ducked out of sight behind the syringa bush but she heard her grandmother's step on the porch floor.

"Here's your mug of coffee, Robert," Grandma said. "Do you know where Flora has disappeared to? She ran off to give Betsy a carrot and she didn't come back to do her dusting."

"Watch out for Fleet. I haven't seen her," Grandpa said. "But she comes by it naturally, wouldn't you say? Her mother was a great one for skipping the dusting, if you remember."

Grandma gave a little snort.

"She had three older sisters ready to spoil her, but she's grown up to be a credit to us."

"I never thought such a harum-scarum youngster would ever make a good minister's wife," she said, resting for a moment perched on the porch railing. "Flora's quieter but she has her mother's gumption. What a glorious morning! It tempts a body into just sitting. But I mustn't. I'll go up and get my thimble and help Margaret out with the darning."

The screen door banged. Grandpa laughed softly and began a third song. "You don't know Nellie well as I do..."

Gorrie had an idea. She dashed around the house, ran in through the kitchen door, snatched up a duster and was hard at work on the legs of the piano stool when her grandmother came back downstairs.

"My, my, what prompted this sudden industry?" she asked.

Gorrie kept her eyes on the duster.

"Satan finds work for idle hands, Grandma," she said in a voice as meek as milk.

William burst into the room.

"Gorrie, I've waited and waited but you never started looking," he complained.

Grandma's lips twitched.

"She couldn't skip the dusting," she said solemnly. "But she can go now. She's worked long enough. Dinner will be ready in half an hour."

She sailed out leaving the children open-mouthed. But Gorrie caught her chuckle before the kitchen door swung shut behind her.

5
Home Missions

Come let us sing of a wonderful love,
Tender and true, tender and true;
Out of the heart of the Father above,
Streaming to me and to you:
Wonderful love, wonderful love
Dwells in the heart of the Father above.
Robert Walmsley

Gorrie stood at the parlour window watching the new snow falling. Supper was over and her mother and Gretta were in the kitchen doing the dishes. She could hear the clink and rattle of plates and cutlery. William was out there too, sitting in the tin tub having a bath and singing "Jingle Bells" at the top of his voice.

She could join them. But there was a crowd there already and she had been drawn to the window by the sight of swirling snowflakes caught in the light from the oil lamp. They were falling so thick and fast they looked like a shining swarm. The brisk wind kept them spinning and dancing.

"Snow bees," Gorrie said softly. Or snow fairies maybe.

Then she saw a towering, dark shape coming toward the front door. It was like nothing she had ever seen and she stopped breathing. It was huge and black and covered with fur. It walked on its hind legs. Bears could do that. Could a bear be carrying something under its arm? She shrank back and opened her mouth to scream when the beast came into the lamplight.

It was a man, a giant of a man in a black fur coat and fur hat pulled low. His face was masked by that hat and by his coat collar, which he had turned up to keep off the biting wind. Even so, after a long moment of disbelief, she knew who the bear-man was.

"Father!" she shrieked and ran for the front door.

They were making such a racket in the kitchen that nobody heard her. She tugged the door wide and in he came, stamping his big boots and blowing the way the horse did when she came into the warmth of the stable.

"Merry Christmas, daughter," he said softly.

She launched herself at him, not minding that he was covered with melting snow. He dropped his burden with a crash and caught her. Safe in his arms, she turned to look at what he had been carrying.

"It's Aunt Nell's little rocker," she said. "Why do you have it?"

"I was there to see them today," her father told her, "and Nell asked me to bring it to you as a Christmas present. She knows how much you love it. I thought you'd be in bed and I was going to hide it but you were too smart for me."

He lowered her to the floor, took off the bearskin coat and cap and draped them over the hat stand. Then he pulled off the snowy boots and stood in his sock feet. Still nobody came. He reached for her hand. Then the big man and the small girl tiptoed down the hall to the kitchen.

Mother turned, caught sight of them and dropped the plate she had been handing to Gretta.

"Will, oh, Will," she shouted out. Then she ran to him and was folded in a bear hug.

Gorrie let go of his hand and backed out of their way.

"I saw him first," she told the others smugly. "I was scared for a minute. I thought he was a bear. He looked exactly like one."

William leapt out of the tub and pranced around the kitchen stark naked and shrieking with excitement. Gretta ran to get hugged next. Grandma, coming to see what all the uproar was about, was scandalized by Will parading around in his birthday suit. She snatched up his nightshirt and gave chase. What a wonderful hullabaloo!

"Why didn't you send us word?" Mother demanded, stepping back and straightening her hair.

"I didn't know just when I could get here and I

thought it would be a surprise. It was nice to spot Flora at the window. I was sure the children would all be in bed."

"It's only seven-thirty. You forget how early darkness comes here in December," his wife said. "I'll go and tell Father that you've come and then I'll get you some supper. Gretta, put the kettle on and slice some bread and meat."

Later, when the whole family, except for baby Dorothy, was gathered around the big kitchen table watching him have his third cup of tea, he told them he would be staying for three or four months. He had meetings to attend and some deputation work to do. He sounded glum about that. Gorrie understood. "Deputation" meant going to churches and asking for money for the missions. He hated asking for money.

"It's for the Lord's work, Will," Mother reminded him now. "It's not as though you're begging for yourself."

"I know. But my salary comes from that money in a roundabout fashion. We have six children, Gret. We clothe and feed them all from what is donated. I sometimes think they believe I should have stayed single if I planned to be a missionary. If you are present, my dear, they understand why I had no choice but to marry, but perhaps six children seems excessive."

Gorrie, beginning to grow sleepy, came awake at that. She liked long words. What did "excessive" mean? She was about to ask when Mother pushed her chair back and began noisily collecting dishes. She banged them together. What had upset her?

"I work hard for the Mission Board when I'm in Tamsui with you," her mother snapped. "And they've never paid me one red cent. They get two missionaries for one salary. And you know quite well that the children are mostly clothed with the hand-me-downs and discards that arrive in those missionary barrels. Gretta has to go to school here wearing dresses her classmates wore and threw away. We bake our own bread and grow our own vegetables and I spend weeks canning fruit and making pickles for the winter. I don't think you need feel like a beggar. They're getting good value for their money."

"You do this speechifying so much better than I do, Gret," he told her more than once in the next few weeks. "You tell your stories and everyone feels as though they've been there. You should have been the preacher instead of me."

"Nonsense," Gorrie's mother said with a pleased laugh. "Remember, William, I didn't even go to high school. You have to correct my English. What sort of preacher makes mistakes in grammar?"

The children knew it was not nonsense. They had often had to listen to both of their parents speak and they infinitely preferred their mother's stirring stories and down-to-earth friendliness to their father's slow, serious sermons. As long as their Chinese clothes fitted them, Gorrie and Gretta were sometimes taken along and dressed up to create atmosphere. Both girls hated having to do this.

"They stare at us as though we're animals in a zoo," Gretta fumed.

Mother shushed her but it was true. Gorrie liked it much better when Mother took them but did not dress them up. Instead, she would get out the tiny cloth shoe made for a woman with bound feet. At least the poor woman who had worn it didn't have to sit there while people talked about her as though she were made of wood. Hearing again and again about how Chinese women bound the feet of little girls close to her own age always made Gorrie shiver.

"If we do nothing else," she heard her mother say many times, "at least we've done our best to stop this barbaric custom. And we've taught girls as well as boys to read. I have several piano students too."

"Oh, Mrs. Gauld, you're too modest. Think of all those poor heathen souls you and your husband have saved from worshipping idols and going straight to Hell," somebody almost always said.

Mother would agree wholeheartedly and then ask someone to pass the collection plate. Money always poured in. Surprisingly, Father was the one to hesitate and look uncomfortable when Canadians talked about the unconverted Formosans as "heathens going straight to Hell." Gorrie felt uncomfortable too. After all, even though Ah Soong was a Christian now, the rest of her family were still Buddhists. Was Ah Soong's sister Nai-yen a heathen? Gorrie supposed so. But it didn't feel right to call her one. She had helped out in the kitchen sometimes and her laugh was so merry it made Gorrie smile just remembering it.

One night in February, they were on their way home from a church service where both her parents had spoken and the girls had worn their Chinese clothes. Gretta and Mother, bundled close together under a buffalo robe, had fallen asleep but Gorrie, sitting next to her father on the driver's seat of the sleigh, was wide awake. It was her chance to ask.

"Would God really send Ah Soong's family to Hell, Father, just because they aren't Christians?"

Father did not say anything for a long moment. Betsy's hooves clip-clopped along the snowy road. A scatter of stars shone down on them. The chiming sleighbells and her father's comfortable bulk beside her made the darkness feel friendly to Gorrie.

"Father…" she began again.

"I heard you," William Gauld said, staring ahead through the horse's ears. "The Bible says people who aren't baptized will go to Hell but it also says God is a God of love. You remember, Flora. His banner over me is love. I can't believe a loving God will punish Ah Soong's family for believing what they were taught from babyhood. But I cannot be sure of the answer. I have to have faith in the mercy of my all-loving Father in Heaven. And I must tell others of that boundless love."

"Oh," was all Gorrie could find to say.

Her father sighed. Then, unexpectedly, he chuckled.

"You've put your finger on a great mystery, daughter," he said. "Why are we sending out missionaries if not to save souls? Sometimes we do harm. Families become divided. But I know Jesus came to show us the love of God. I cannot bear it that people live in fear, never having heard of that love."

Gorrie slid her hand in under his elbow. She felt as though, for one moment, she was the grown-up and he was the child.

"Come let us sing of a wonderful love," she quoted to him, "tender and true, tender and true."

Father let go of the reins with his left hand and patted her gloved fingers.

"That's it," he said. "I must try to translate that hymn into Taiwanese. It says it all."

When they got home, Gorrie went straight to bed. She snuggled down and stretched her feet out across the whole mattress. Once Gretta came up, she would have less than half the space. She felt comforted and cosy. She would not bring up the subject of hellfire when she was alone with Mother. Father's slow, thoughtful words had given her peace.

When spring came, Father went back to Taiwan without them. Gorrie missed him sorely at first. She felt so safe with him. And he never laughed at her or repeated one of her questions to company, calling them "Flora's quaint sayings," as her mother did. The older she got, the more surely Gorrie learned never to ask Mother a question that mattered. "If God so loves the little sparrow, why doesn't he keep it from falling in the first place?" was one of the puzzles that worried Gorrie but amused her mother. Mother thought Gorrie was comical when she was being deadly serious.

One night, after they had been dressed up in their Chinese outfits once too often, the two girls decided they had had enough. Gorrie came upon Gretta sticking scissors into the front of the jacket she had to wear.

"What are you doing?" she whispered, shocked and delighted because she had already guessed.

"I heard Mother say she would have to let them out so they'd go on fitting us," Gretta said, driving the points of her scissors into the cloth.

Gorrie ran for the ink bottle. She knew, from sad experience, that once you spilled this ink on clothing, the stain was impossible to get out. She splashed some on the knee of the pants and across the front of the jacket. As she did so, she remembered how Ah Soong had loved seeing them in these outfits. But she was sure that Ah Soong would have understood if she had ever sat and watched them being shown off to raise money for "the heathen."

Mother opened the door and walked in on them just as they finished. Both girls blushed guiltily and ducked their heads, braced for a storm. But, to their astonishment, Mother understood too. She picked up the ruined clothes, sighed and then bundled them into the rag bag.

"You've done your share," she told her daughters. "I really knew it was time we stopped getting you up this way. It's just that it makes people see that there are real children in Taiwan who need help."

"You tell them, Mother," Gretta said. "They'll believe you."

"Yes," Gorrie said. She thought about the real Taiwanese people she loved and had left behind. Ah Soong's smile flashed before her mind's eye and brought a lump to her throat. She ran for paper and ink and a pen.

"Gretta, help me write Ah Soong a letter."

Gretta put aside the sewing scissors and picked up the pen.

"What shall I say?" she asked.

"Say 'Dearest Ah Soong, We miss you so much. We often wish you were here.'"

"Do you really?"

"Really what?" Gorrie asked.

"Really miss her so much and wish she were here?"

"Yes," said Gorrie Gauld simply. "I do."

6
Joining Daniel's Band

◈

Dare to be a Daniel.
Dare to stand alone!
Dare to have a purpose firm!
Dare to make it known.
Philip P. Bliss

Con White came over at two o'clock, knowing Gorrie would have finished her Saturday morning chores by then and be free to play. Gorrie ran to let her in. Without speaking a word, she led the way to the parlour door. They weren't usually allowed to play in this holy of holies but Grandma and Mother had been persuaded that they needed a stretch of carpet where they could spread out this particular game. They also needed to be private. Will or even Gretta shifting anything or making fun of the game could rob it of its delight.

"We'll tidy up every scrap afterwards," Gorrie

promised each time.

"Edith asked me again what we're doing," Con reported with a grin, "and Nettie begged to come. I felt sorry for Nettie but she'd wreck everything. And Edith wouldn't understand."

"No," Gorrie said. She crawled in behind the settee for their supplies and emerged with an outdated copy of Eaton's catalogue and a large dented hat box, which looked shabby to the adults but gorgeous to the girls. Removing the lid of the round hat box, she pulled out a neatly folded, large, white cotton handkerchief.

"I've got a new one," she said. "It was Grandpa's. He got ink on one corner and Grandma couldn't get it out. It's not a big spot but he won't use it."

The two girls laid out their houses, each room being a handkerchief spread flat on the carpet. Then they added bits of cut-up hair ribbon for furniture. Grandpa's handkerchief became the schoolhouse. As they chose new families from the catalogue, cut them out, named them and discussed how they were related and what sort of people they were, they became totally absorbed. A few minutes into the game, Gorrie began searching the catalogue for a schoolteacher.

"Should it be a woman or a man?" she asked.

"A woman," Con said at once. "We wouldn't want the children to have a man teacher like Mr. Forster."

"Is he really so awful? Gretta hates him, I know,

but Harvey says he wasn't all that bad."

"He likes boys better than girls, that's one reason," Con told her, sitting back on her heels to think this over. "He keeps on at Gretta about Gordon and Harvey being so much smarter than she is. He's really mean to her. She wouldn't make so many mistakes if he didn't get her hot and bothered. You're lucky not to have to go to school this year."

Gorrie made a face.

"I don't feel lucky. I want to go more than anything. I think they're going to let me go this fall. Will went last year and he's only six—more than a year younger than me. It's not fair."

"My mother says your mother thought you were too sickly or something," Con put in. "Frail. That's what she said."

Gorrie sprang up and marched up and down, her cheeks red, her eyes stormy, her dark hair bouncing on the back of her neck.

"I'm every bit as tough as William," she declared. "I just didn't grow as fast. It's not my fault I'm small. I finally let them all know that I can read. That helped. They were so surprised."

She giggled and dropped down to the carpet again. Picking out a kind-faced lady in a shirtwaist and navy skirt, she began cutting her out with care.

Con stared at her in fascination.

"You mean you could read and you kept it a secret?"

Gorrie looked up at her friend's round eyes and laughed softly.

"Yes. I started learning before I turned five and I could read whole books a year ago," she said, cutting around the teacher's feet.

"Why didn't you tell? How did you ever keep them from guessing? I'd have let it out for sure."

"I like listening to people reading aloud. Gretta couldn't read well until she was seven or eight. I can remember them saying, 'You read to yourself, young lady. It'll be good practice.' I didn't want that to happen to me. They did catch me reading once in awhile but I pretended I was looking at the pictures or I asked them to tell me a simple word."

"Wasn't that kind of like...lying?" Con asked, not looking at her friend.

"If they'd asked me right out, I'd have told them," Gorrie said, putting the teacher down at the front of the schoolroom. "I didn't mean to keep it a secret so long. Gretta guessed, of course, but she didn't tell. Now I wish I'd told them long ago. They might have sent me to school last year with William."

"Maybe you'll change your mind when you get there and then it will be too late. You'll hate arithmetic."

"Maybe I will and maybe I won't," Gorrie said, thinking of all she had learned helping out in the store and Post Office. She liked the neatness of numbers and felt at home with them in a way Gretta never did. She could already make change if it weren't more than a dollar.

"Look at this child," Con said with a laugh.

"She's so little and sweet. I'm going to call her Flora and put her in the tiny pink bedroom."

Gorrie glanced at the toddler dressed in ruffles and wearing a gigantic hair ribbon.

"Don't you dare," she said. "She's a Dora maybe. If you call any child Flora, she won't sleep in a tiny pink room. She'll want green maybe. Or white with flowers in the corner like that one."

Finally came the September day that Gorrie had longed for ever since her sixth birthday. She looked down with deep satisfaction at the plaid dress Grandma had made her. It was from an old kilt that had belonged to Father, the tartan of the Gordons. It made her feel linked with him, even though she suspected he would not approve of a kilt being turned into a little girl's dress.

The important thing was that nobody at Tuckersmith School would have seen it before. On her first day, at least, she would not have to wear somebody's hand-me-down. She had new hair ribbons too. She had run them lovingly through her fingers countless times in the last week, exulting in their satiny sheen and smoothness. They would never look quite so lovely again, she knew. They were a deep green and one and a half inches wide.

Mother tied them carefully, pulling them as tight as she could since Gorrie was famous for losing hair ribbons. She had on her long white stockings and her patent leather Sunday shoes. Tomorrow she'd be back in tan stockings and her scuffed brown boots. But this day was special.

All the Kippen girls started out together, the older ones slowing their pace so that younger sisters and timid little brothers could keep up. Gorrie felt they were like a marching parade. She wanted to burst into song. But she was suddenly shy. Also she was concentrating on keeping her shoes shiny. It wasn't easy with the road so dusty.

"I hate going back," she heard her sister muttering to her friend Winnifred.

"Not me," Winnifred said. "If I had to stay home, I'd have to help with the last of the canning. The jars look wonderful when they're full and standing in a row but it's such hot work and you never get to stop for a rest. Besides, I haven't seen Billy Harding all summer."

Gretta snorted.

"You'll never catch me mooning over some boy," she said. "I sort of like canning if it isn't too hot."

Gorrie felt sorry for Winnifred. There were nine children and four grown-ups in her family and the amount of preserving her mother and aunt did was legendary.

The two and a half miles Mother had thought would wear her frail little Flora out were gone in a twinkling. There was so much to see on the way, so many jokes to tell, such gossip to catch and pass on.

And it was such a glorious morning. The sky was deep blue. As Gorrie walked along, staring up, she felt she was taken up into it and flew, for one magic instant. Although some leaves were still green, many had turned scarlet or buttery yellow. Birds sang everywhere. A V-shaped line of geese, heading south, honked a wild greeting from high above. Two black squirrels chased each other along a fence rail and up a leaning birch tree, shouting friendly insults at each other as they ran.

Then one perfect maple leaf came spinning down to light softly on Gorrie's shoulder. She took it in her fingers and carried it along for luck. She would press it between the pages of her Bible and keep it forever.

"Hurry, Gretta," she called softly to her sister. "I can't wait."

"I can," her sister growled, but she walked a little more briskly.

Everyone got to school in lots of time and there was plenty of excitement as children greeted friends and yelled at enemies they had not seen all summer long. Then Mr. Forster came out and rang the bell.

"Flora Gauld, you may sit with Nettie Baines," the teacher said in his abrupt way after everyone had filed into the one-room schoolhouse.

Gorrie slid into her side of the double desk, feeling like a proper scholar at last. She got out her new pencil box and took out the fat pink eraser and one of the three brand new pencils Grandpa had sharpened for her with his whittling knife. She put the pencil in the trough meant for pencils and beamed at it.

When it was time for her to read aloud, she stood up very straight and read without hesitation through the selection Mr. Forster indicated.

"Hmm," he said, frowning slightly. "Try this."

She was in the Fifth Reader before she stumbled over a word.

"Well, well, another Gauld with plenty of brains," the teacher said, sending a sneering glance at Gretta, three rows behind her.

Stricken by his cutting remark, Gorrie looked back. Was Gretta hurt?

Her sister smiled at her. Her cheeks were flushed and her eyes looked suspiciously bright but she was clearly proud of Gorrie's ability. Gorrie sat down and waited for the arithmetic lesson. She turned out to be ahead of the other students her age not only in Reading but in Spelling, Grammar, Arithmetic and History. She had never tried to learn to write so her penmanship was that of a beginner.

"Your sister's handwriting is abysmal," the teacher said. "You must not take her as your model."

Gorrie wanted to contradict him but she couldn't. She had heard Mother complain about Gretta's illegible writing. Also, despite herself, she was already a little afraid of the man who ruled Tuckersmith School.

Having new books to read and new friends to play with at recess made school fun at first, but Gorrie soon came to realize that all the students, even the biggest boys like Ned Baines and Dan Baker, were afraid of the teacher, whether they admitted it or not. The children had to move carefully and keep watching him out of the corners of their eyes for signs of trouble.

One day, Gorrie slid a glance in his direction and saw him jerk open the drawer of his desk. He pulled out a bottle, took a quick swig from it and dropped it back out of sight. Little Pearl Nesbit, who was barely six and a bit simple, must have been gazing at him openly for his black eyebrows drew together in an ominous way. He gave one of his rasping coughs and patted his chest.

"It's my medicine," he growled. "My cough medicine."

Then he shoved his chair back so violently that it banged the chalk trough. The entire class jumped. Their teacher strode over to the high window. Hands clasped behind his back, right foot drumming on the floor, he stared out at the fields. His fields.

They all knew he would rather be out working on his farm than cooped up with them in the school. Yet proud as he was of his land, Mr. Forster was a poor farmer and took the teaching job to make payments on his many debts. Every child sitting before him knew he owed money to the blacksmith and the grocer, the feed store and the doctor. No adult had told them so outright but they had overheard things and, comparing the scraps they gathered, pieced together the truth.

"Quiet," he rasped suddenly, swinging around to glare at them.

The room was deathly still. Every head bent studiously over a book and everyone but Pearl held his or her breath. Who would he pick on this time?

Not Gretta, Gorrie prayed, not Gretta again.

It wasn't only Gretta who set him off. He lost his temper over trifles—a dropped pencil, a whispered remark, a smothered giggle. The big boys had to watch their step. He had switched them all by now, making them cut the switch themselves and sending them back out if the thin whippy branches weren't to his liking. Gorrie had come close to vomiting while she sat through this. He didn't hurt them so very badly, they claimed afterward, but he was like a giant cat playing with mice.

The boys knew better than to tell on him. Their parents would be likely to give them a second licking to match the teacher's. He had not yet switched a girl though. No parent was likely to tolerate that.

With the girls, he resorted to biting sarcasm or humiliation. Standing Florrie Makepeace or Susan Fowler in the corner with a dunce cap on her head always reduced them to floods of tears. As soon as they began to weep, he smiled and was kind. Both Florrie and Susan had learned to burst into sobs the moment he turned on them.

But Gretta Gauld was made of sterner stuff. However she felt inside, she was too proud to cry. Her furious silence and stubborn chin drove Mr. Forster to a frenzy. She was the only girl he had struck and he had been careful even then to give her palms just a couple of licks with his ruler and then quit.

"Tell Mother," Gorrie had said that afternoon.

Gretta shook her head wearily.

"She'd say it was my fault," she said. "Maybe I really am stupid. I can't tell."

"I'll tell her myself," Gorrie said, hot with anger on her sister's behalf. Gretta got the worst bullying of all.

"No. Don't. I'll try harder," Gretta said, looking miserable. "I couldn't bear it if she were ashamed of me."

Mother had been away that evening making a speech and Gretta managed to keep Grandma from seeing her reddened palms. By the following night, the marks had disappeared.

Gorrie was pondering this, staring out the window, when her teacher's voice brought her up sharp.

"Flora Gauld, get to work at once. You'll fall as far behind as your sister, if you let yourself sit there staring into space that way."

Gorrie looked at Mr. Forster, one steady brave look, and went back to her arithmetic. One of these days, he would go too far and she would tell on him, whatever her sister said. Thinking about it, she shivered. But she had made up her mind.

She did not have to wait long. A week later, just as she was spooning in her last bite of oatmeal, Gretta burst out, "Mother, how can I make Gord stop flicking water at me? He's so mean."

Gorrie was startled at the raw fury in her sister's voice. She knew exactly what Gretta meant. Whenever either girl went near the bucket of water on the shelf just inside the back door leading out of the kitchen, Gordon would dip his fingertips into the water and flick it at her.

Gorrie just did her best to duck. She even thought it was funny sometimes. But Gretta was driven mad by it.

"You'll have to settle it yourself, daughter," Mother said calmly, slicing bread. "If I were you, I'd wait my chance and pay him back in his own coin. That boy needs a lesson."

She was serious, Gorrie knew, but she also adored her oldest son. "Gret, you think the sun, moon and stars rise and set on that boy," Grandma Mellis had said. "It isn't good for him." But her tart words changed nothing. Mother's face lighted up whenever Gordon came through the door.

At that moment, he came clattering down the back stairs into the kitchen, all set to grab a hasty breakfast and leave for Seaforth. He walked too near the bucket which Harvey had just filled at the backyard pump.

Gorrie's eyes widened as she saw her older sister grab the dipper, fill it to the brim and let fly at her tormenter. At the last second, Gordon saw the danger. His arm jerked up. The dipper went spinning through the air. And both Gordon and Gretta were soaked to the skin.

"What on earth...?" Gord spluttered, mopping water from his face. "Have you gone mad, Gretta?"

"My stars!" Mother exclaimed, swinging around with the breadknife upraised.

And poor wet Gretta got even wetter by bursting

into a storm of tears. Mother was not the only one who idolized the eldest of the Gaulds. Gretta, infuriated by his teasing as she was, worshipped him too.

Mother took a long look at the dripping pair and burst into gales of laughter. Gorrie smiled a little. Grandma Mellis was scandalized both by Gretta's rash act and by her daughter's unseemly mirth. Grandpa, who had caught a few flying drops, shook his beard and murmured, "Very refreshing." That had been enough to set Mother off again.

It had taken awhile to get the two combatants into dry clothes. Will went ahead with his friends but Gorrie waited for her sister to come bounding down the back stairs.

Mother put out her hand and caught her daughter by the shoulder.

"That blouse fits you a little too snugly, my girl. You are filling out faster than I realized. Perhaps you should go back upstairs and..."

"I can't!" Gretta howled. "We'll be late as it is."

"He can't eat you," her mother said calmly, never having seen Mr. Forster in a rage. "Oh, all right. But don't put it on again until I see if it can be let out."

From the moment they left home and saw no other child on the road ahead of them, the two girls knew they were going to be late. Even though the schoolhouse was more than two miles away, Gretta began to run.

"Gorrie, hurry. You're going to make us later than late. Mr. Forster will be mad as a hive of hornets," she called over her shoulder.

Flora Gauld heard the desperate urgency in her sister's voice but it was as though it came from a long way away.

She was kicking a stone down the dusty road. It was an especially nice stone, with a reddish stripe across it, but its jerky journey along the dirt road was covering it with dust so that it would soon look like any old pebble. Maybe she should rescue it.

She stooped down but, as her fingertips curled to grasp it, Gretta grabbed her by her elbow and yanked her upright. Gorrie's free hand flashed out and snatched up the pebble, though, and she had it, safe and sound, in her left fist. Gretta might think she was the boss but that stone was Gorrie's.

"Oh, no!"

"What is it?" Gorrie asked.

Then she saw. The middle button on Gretta's blouse had popped off in their short tussle. Now it was Gretta's turn to swoop down to retrieve something. Then, wordlessly, the pair of them ran hell for leather toward the schoolhouse. Yet, long before they reached it, both girls saw that the doors were closed.

"Oh, Gorrie," the older girl moaned. "Why couldn't you have run?"

Gorrie knew they would have been late however quickly they had raced the two and a half miles but she kept mum. Her sister had enough to bear. Without needing to talk about it, they practically tiptoed up the path, making as little stir as possible.

They eased open the Girls' Door and slid their bodies through the crack. Their coats flew onto hooks without a sound and they started toward their desks without raising their eyes from the floor. It was useless.

"You are tardy," the grating voice announced. "Flora Gauld, you may take your seat next to Nettie. No, wait."

Gorrie turned to face the teacher. She raised her chin, locked her knees so that he would not see them shake and tried to meet his stare. She clutched the striped stone so tightly that she felt its rough corners bite into her palm. Was he going to send her outside to cut a switch? He had never done such a thing to a girl, let alone a girl as small as she, but he looked so terrifying.

"Turn your face to the light, girl."

She did. Why were his gooseberry green eyes raking across her face and throat that way? His beefy hand reached out and pulled her collar away from her neck.

"Mr. Forster," Gretta half-shouted, "it wasn't her fault."

She sprang forward, unaware of her blouse gaping open as she did so, showing her camisole, and put an arm around Gorrie. The teacher's gaze raked her from head to foot, stopping one second on her missing button. Then he gave an ugly laugh.

"Well, Miss Flora, you can turn yourself around and march right back home," he said. "Tell your mother to take a closer look at her offspring next

time before she sends them here to give their dis-
eases to others. You have the German measles."

Gorrie did not move. German measles? What
was he talking about? There was nothing wrong
with her.

"She can't have..." her sister said, pulling her
around to look.

"Even *you* must be able to see those spots," he
jeered. "I haven't forgotten your lateness. Go along,
Flora."

"I'll go with her," Gretta said, putting her arm
back around her. "Mother wouldn't want her to go
alone. She's only..."

"Take your seat, miss," the man thundered at her.
"You need extra drill, not holiday walks. Your sister
is old enough to return down a straight road. She
has spots, not galloping consumption. SIT DOWN!"

"I'm all right," Gorrie told her sister and bolted
out of the schoolhouse.

As she headed down the long road again, she
rubbed away hot tears. How could he be so mean to
Gretta? Gorrie hated him as she had never hated
anyone in her life before.

Then, with a sickening jolt, she forgot her sister's
troubles. She was going to have to walk through the
woods all alone.

It was a long stretch of dense bush halfway
between her and home. The tangled trees crowded
together right to the fence. In that woods, an old
woman, wearing rags and bent double, prowled
and muttered. Boys who, on dares, had gone close

enough to hear some of what she said, swore she talked of eating children and casting spells. The grown-ups called her Biddy Flynn and gave her food sometimes, and cast-off clothes.

"Poor old thing," they said.

But every child attending Tuckersmith School, even those as old as Gretta, knew for sure that she was a witch.

And that was not all. Mother herself had warned them about the tramps who sat in the fence corners. The children weren't allowed to talk to them and were told to walk briskly by and stay together. Gorrie had a sick feeling. She knew they stole away children her size and put them in workhouses or sold them to gypsies.

She turned to run back. Then, remembering poor Gretta, she swung around again and went doggedly forward.

It seemed only seconds until she reached the long stretch of road between the dark, crowding tangle of trees.

"I could run," she said in a trembling voice.

Then she felt the hard stone bite into her palm. Why this gave her courage she never knew, but she did not run.

She began to sing instead. She sang at the top of her voice and marched fast but deliberately down the long, long road.

> Many giants, great and tall,
> Stalking thro' the land,

Headlong to the earth would fall
If met by Daniel's Band.

When she reached the end of the hymn, she was nearly halfway home. She did not pause to look behind or even to the side. She sang on:

Onward! Christian soldiers,
Marching as to war,
With the Cross of Jesus
Going on before.
Christ, the royal Master,
Leads against the foe;
Forward into battle,
See! His banners go.

All at once, the woods were behind her. To her astonishment, she realized that she had started enjoying herself before she was in the clear. She didn't really feel sick. And she had the whole day, maybe a week even, free from Mr. Forster's classroom. She would read and read and read. Today she would finish *The Little Lame Prince*. Even if they thought she shouldn't strain her eyes, she would manage it somehow.

And she would tell the grown-ups about the way Mr. Forster treated her sister. She had already tried, but she had a feeling that, this time, they might listen.

She was on the last page of her book when the other children came home. And she didn't have to tell Mother. Gretta stumbled in, looking sicker than her little sister ever had.

And there were big red welts all over her arms and legs.

"Why, Gretta, whatever happened?" Grandma asked. "What did you do?"

Gretta tried to talk but she was crying too hard.

"She couldn't say the seven times table," Nellie White, Con's big sister said. "Honestly, Mrs. Mellis, that was all it was. She kept making mistakes because he yelled about Gordon and Harvey and Flora being so smart. Then he said she wasn't decent and he just went crazy and grabbed up a switch he'd used on Fred Barker and started hitting her. Only he didn't stop after a couple of licks. He kept hitting her until Pearl began to howl. Then he stopped. It was four o'clock but nobody dared move. Then he yelled, 'Get out, all of you!' and went for his cough medicine bottle. It was awful."

Mother sat holding Gretta, even though she was nearly twelve. She looked sick. And Gretta, limp in her arms, reminded Gorrie of a broken doll.

"There's a school board meeting tonight. You must go, Gret, and tell them," Grandma said. "There's no excuse for such behaviour."

"I'll go," Gorrie's mother said grimly, "and I'll take Gretta with me so that they can see for themselves. And she won't set foot in that place until he's gone."

"I'll go with you," Grandpa said in a hard voice none of the children had heard him use before.

Gorrie looked at her sister's face. No delight sprang up in her eyes. No switch could have hurt her this deeply. It had taken all the weeks of cutting words and sneering looks beforehand.

She had no doubt that her mother and her grandfather could and would rid them of their teacher forever. Her mother, once roused, was like a tigress defending her cubs. Mr. Forster's days at Tuckersmith School were almost over. But his going might not be enough.

It's too late, Gorrie thought. I ought to have told long ago. She will never be able to forget the things he said about her. Daring to be a Daniel sounded simple. It wasn't simple at all.

She went over to stand beside her sister. And she took out her special striped stone and dropped it into Gretta's pocket. It just might bring her a bit of luck.

7
Happy Sid

◈

There were ninety and nine that safely lay
In the shelter of the fold;
But one was out on the hills away,
Far off from the gates of gold,
Away on the mountain wild and bare,
Away from the tender Shepherd's care.
Elizabeth Cecilia Clephane

Gorrie was playing with her doll Gertrude on the plank walk in front of the Mellis house when Happy Sid came along. She looked up at him and, seeing he was nobody she knew, her casual glance changed to a wide-eyed stare. Rarely did a stranger walk through Kippen, let alone a stranger with eyes as blue as cornflowers and a smile that made you have to smile back.

"Hello, little girl," he said, sweeping off his battered cap so that his fair hair gleamed in the morning sunshine. "What's your name?"

Gorrie hesitated. Then she made up her mind he was a friend.

"My proper name is Flora Gauld," she told him.

"And your improper one?" He laughed as he asked and Gorrie had to smile too.

"Almost everybody calls me Gorrie."

He glanced at the house. Grandpa was on the verandah not fifty feet from where they were talking but he was sound asleep. His head lolled against the back of his chair, his snowy beard was pointed at the porch roof and he was snoring rhythmically. Gorrie decided he would like to meet the stranger.

"What's your name?" she asked in a low voice. "I'll introduce you to Grandpa. You'll have to take his hand to shake it because he can't see."

"Aha," said the man, also speaking softly. "I'd like to meet Mr. Gauld. I think I'm a friend of your uncle's. I'm not positive though. His name's John, isn't it?"

Gorrie shot him a surprised look.

"Grandpa's not Mr. Gauld, he's Mr. Mellis," she said. "And my Uncle John died before I was born. You must mean Uncle Will. He used to live in Lucknow but he went to Mexico. He and his wife and their little girl got typhoid fever and they died."

"Of course your grandfather's name is Mellis," the stranger agreed, looking sheepish. "Don't you tell him I got it wrong. Hearing your name is Gauld mixed me up. And it was your Uncle Will who was my friend. I've been away and I hadn't heard about his death. What a tragedy! I'm glad I stopped though to meet you all before I go on to Wingham."

Satisfied by this lengthy speech, Gorrie led the way up the front path. As the stranger approached the steps, Fleet, aging but on guard, growled.

"Hush, Fleet. Grandpa," she called, tapping the old man softly on one knee, "Grandpa, wake up. A friend of Uncle Will's has come to see you."

Grandpa jumped and then said uncertainly, "What is it, child?"

Fleet put his head back down but did his best to keep an eye on the person he did not know. The fair-haired man gave the dog a look Gorrie could not read and then leaned forward and took Robert Mellis's hand in his firm grasp, just as Gorrie had told him to.

"You won't have heard of me, Mr. Mellis," he said in a warm pleasing voice. "But I was a friend of your son Will before he went to Mexico. I was travelling this way and thought I'd drop in to see Will's family. My name is Sidney Tanner but I'm called Happy Sid since I found the Lord and was saved."

Grandpa Mellis smiled up at the friendly voice.

"Flora," he said to Gorrie, "run inside and tell your grandmother and your mother about Mr. Tanner. I hope you'll give us the pleasure of sharing our noon meal with us, sir."

Gorrie was about to run into the house when Happy Sid's next words made it impossible for her to leave.

"I saw a man hanged at dawn today," he said

quietly, sinking into the big chair next to Grandpa's, "and I'm grateful for the respite. I spent all night in his cell praying with him, wrestling for his soul. I rejoice to say he too was saved by the blood of the Lamb before he went to his God. The struggle was worth it, well worth it, but it taxed my strength. It is healing to be with a loving family for an hour or so after such a harrowing experience."

"Run along, Flora," Grandpa said firmly.

She moved off, no longer surprised at her grand-father's awareness of what went on near his chair. It was hard to tear herself away but she managed it. When she reached the kitchen, the story all came out in such a jumble that both women put down their work to go and check. Gorrie followed at their heels.

"I was with him when he died," Sid was saying solemnly. "His last words were, 'Lord, forgive me for all my wickedness.' It did our hearts good to hear him."

"Was he a murderer?" Gorrie burst out before Grandpa could introduce Mr. Tanner to his wife and daughter. Happy Sid gave them a look of apology and answered her seriously, almost as though she were a grown-up.

"He was indeed. He had stabbed a fellow in a brawl at the tavern and the man died. He bitterly repented this act but it was too late."

"Are you yourself a drinking man, Mr. Tanner?" Grandma asked the moment her husband finished the introductions.

Gorrie held her breath. If Sid were a drunkard, Grandma would not have him in the house except to sober him up.

"Whisky is the Devil in solution," she was fond of thundering.

Gorrie understood the bit about the Devil but she did not know what "in solution" meant. She watched her new friend with anxious eyes. Fleet raised his head again, as if he too wanted to know the answer.

"Once I was a sorry case, Mrs. Mellis," Sid said in a low sad voice. "Until I accepted Jesus Christ as my Saviour, I went to bed drunk most nights. But now I'm in the Saved Army and I go about doing the Lord's work. He showed me a better way and gave me the strength I needed to cling to it. I can say today that no liquor has passed my lips since the day I found God."

Gorrie thrilled to his words. She had sung about sinners all her life and heard of people who changed their ways from evil to good. But she had never seen a real one close up like this. He was so handsome, so friendly and so good. And she, Gorrie Gauld, had seen him first.

Fleet growled softly again and his hackles lifted but nobody paid any attention.

"Did you know Will in Lucknow?" Grandpa Mellis asked.

"I did indeed," Sid said. "I heard him speak of you many times in those years. I was saddened to hear of his passing from Flora here. I've been away

from those parts for several years. I'm out of touch
with the folks at home. I'm going that way soon to
set things right between us while I have the chance.
I should have asked their forgiveness first of all."

Gorrie watched his face intently. He looked so
sorry for the sorrow he had caused. She knew about
that kind of sorrow. Their house stood right across
the road from the tavern. When Grandma saw a
man thrown out the door late at night, she would
get Mother and the two of them would go out and
heave him up off the road and bring him in. A pot of
strong coffee would be brewing on the stove for the
purpose of sobering the luckless man up. Mother
had objected to this procedure every so often.

"It would serve him right to spend the night in
the ditch," she would say.

"It surely would," Grandma would answer. "But
he wouldn't wake up there, Gret. One of his cronies
would hoist him into a buggy or up on a horse and
they'd drop him off at his own front door. And he'd
be so drunk and so ashamed of himself that he'd
black his wife's eye or beat a child who gave him an
accusing look. I've seen it happen often. On Sunday,
she'd stay home from church or come wearing her
heaviest veil to hide the marks of his fist. It's never
for the drunkard's own sake that I pluck him out of
the gutter. I do it for the poor woman and innocent
children who have to bear his brutish behaviour
when he arrives home drunk."

Watching Happy Sid with worshipful eyes all
through the noon meal and then into the afternoon,

Gorrie tried to imagine him like one of those slumped and sorry men she had glimpsed, crying, in the kitchen.

It was impossible. This lovely man could never have staggered like that, talking loudly and foolishly about all the men he had worsted in fist fights or sobbing about the women who had brought him to this pitiful state. Those men were disgusting. Sometimes they even threw up on themselves or wet their pants. Gretta had told her about the pants. However bad he had been, she could not believe that Sidney would ever have acted so disgracefully.

He stayed on for supper. They ate in state in the dining room. Fleet, still snappish, was exiled to the kitchen.

"He's getting old, Mr. Tanner. You'll have to forgive him," Grandma said. "He's usually such a good-tempered dog."

Just as Mother was getting the mailbag locked up, ready to carry to the train station, their visitor said he had to check which train he should take and offered to carry the mailbag along. Mother hesitated. It was the responsibility of the Village Postmaster, in this case herself, to deliver the locked mailbag to the station.

"I didn't mean to be presuming," Sid said humbly. "I just thought I could save you a trip. But don't trust me if you have the slightest doubt."

"Let him do it, Gret," her father said. "You've worked hard all day. It's not as though it weren't safely locked."

"I'll be back soon," Sid said and disappeared, carrying the heavy mailbag over his shoulder.

Gorrie could feel a slight tension in the house.

"I hope he really is as honest as he claims," Mother muttered uneasily, going to the window. "Fleet's growling that way made me wonder a little."

"He was so sincere, Mother," Gretta said. "Think of him being up all night with that poor man and then seeing him hanged!"

Gorrie felt sick, remembering that man. She found she was glad Happy Sid had never told them the murderer's name. His being nameless made it a bit more unreal, a little easier to bear.

"Here he comes," Will sang out. "Howdy, Sid."

"William, you call Mr. Tanner by his surname. Show some respect," Grandma snapped.

"I'll have to ask to sleep on the hay in your barn, I'm afraid," Sid said cheerfully. "I discovered that I can't catch my train until morning. Besides, I admit I feel the need of a good night's sleep."

"You can bed down on the couch in the kitchen," Gorrie's grandmother said slowly. "No need to sleep in the hay."

They had a happy evening. Sid regaled them with stories of people he had known and he coaxed Grandpa into playing his concertina while everyone sang. Then Mother went to the parlour organ and some of the neighbours even came to join in the hymn sing. They started at the front of the hymn book and went through, singing everybody's favourites.

"That's my life story," Sid said solemnly when they came to "Amazing Grace."

"Where's the mailbag key?" Mother asked just as everyone was going to bed.

They all looked at the nail on which it always hung. It wasn't there. Mother searched the floor. No key. Sid joined in the hunt but it did not turn up.

"Leave it till daylight, daughter," Grandpa said at last. "Someone must have brushed against it and knocked it down and then it got kicked into a corner or something. It'll turn up."

"At least I locked the mailbag safely before it was mislaid," Mother said. But the relief in her voice did not disguise the underlying worry.

"Good-night," they all said to Sid.

Gorrie went over to him and touched his hand shyly.

"I saw you first," she whispered.

He leaned down and looked into her wide hazel eyes. His look was sad.

"Remember me kindly, little Gorrie," he said. "I wish, for your sake, that I were the man you think I am."

He spoke so softly only Gorrie heard him. She smiled and ran off up the stairs. She would see him in the morning.

Grandma was the first one down, as usual, but it was Gretta who saw the mailbag key back on its hook.

"Where was the key?" she asked.

Grandma stared at it.

"I have no idea," she said slowly.

Gorrie, running down the stairs, called out, "Where's Sid?"

Nobody answered. She thought the silence was a reproof to her for being overfamiliar with their guest.

"Where's Mr. Tanner?" she said quickly, hoping to escape a lecture.

Gretta had already sped out the door to look around. She came back white-faced.

"He's gone," she said, "and I found these. They've been opened." Mutely she held out three envelopes which had been opened and discarded. The adults recognized them. Each one had contained a mortgage payment.

Gorrie refused to believe it. She shouted at them that they were being unfair. She wept hot tears as she sought to defend him. Then, all at once, she remembered the last thing he had said to her and she knew it was true. He had delivered the locked mailbag but he had taken the key first. He had gone through the letters looking for money before handing over the bag. Gorrie felt utterly betrayed and heartsick.

"Fleet tried to tell us. If we'd just listened to him! And if only we knew where he was going," her grandmother said, "we could call the police and have him picked up."

"What will they do to him if they catch him?" Will asked excitedly.

Gorrie was glad he had asked. She needed to

know. Waiting for the answer, she felt taut as a fiddle string.

"He'd go to jail for a few months, I suppose," Mother said dully. "But it's no use talking about it. He was careful not to tell us where he was bound. We can't give the police any help."

"He was going to Wingham," Gorrie whispered. "He told me when we were outside."

They telegraphed the police in Wingham. Then Mother said she must go to London to report on what had happened.

"Today's a holiday," Grandma said. "Nobody will be there until tomorrow morning. The Post Office isn't like the police station."

"Tomorrow will be soon enough, Gret. I'll ask Tom to check Betsy's shoes before you go," Grandpa put in. "Don't take this too hard, daughter. Remember that this isn't the first attempt on the Post Office. It happened before you were married, if you recall, and once again while Jen was with us. That time, the thieves took some of my best socks!"

The family laughed at his outraged tone, knowing he was trying to lighten the gloom.

Tom Mellis came over at daylight and took Betsy to the smithy. Gorrie and William went along, happy to watch the iron shoes being forged and nailed to their horse's hooves. Gorrie gazed at Tom wonderingly. They all knew his history. He had come to Canada as a ten-year-old Barnardo boy and had been adopted by their grandfather. Grandpa had had his sight then and was still the village blacksmith. He was the one who had taught Tom all he knew of the smith's work.

"Is it true, Tom, that you don't know what your last name was before you came here?" she asked, hoping to be told the story again.

The tall man grinned down at her uplifted face.

"You know the answer to that one, missy," he said. "I was a street lad. I can't remember having parents or ever sleeping under a roof I could call home. Then Dr. Barnardo came by, just as three of us were being taken up for stealing, and he took us all to his Home."

"What sort of home did he have?" asked William.

"I mean his orphans' home. The lads called me Tom. I knew of no other name. Next thing I knew, Dr. Barnardo was asking me if I wanted to make a fresh start in Canada. I'd never heard of Canada. I thought it must be some other Home he had, outside of London, so I says I'd go. I had a full belly for the first time in my life, and clothes that weren't rags, and kindness. Some of the lads ran away first chance they got but I stuck it, being more than ready for a new life. I was only ten, younger than Gretta. Out of the way now. William, get back or you'll get your hair singed off."

William leaped back. Gorrie laughed, forgetting Happy Sid as she tried to picture raggedy little Tom.

"Go on," she begged, the moment he was free to speak.

"Well, they gave me a trunk with a change of clothes and my own Bible which I still have. Then a huge crowd of us marched, like little soldiers, to the ship. I was still in a muddle. As the ship pulled away, one chap, half a head taller than me, yelled out, 'Goodbye to you, old England. May we never starve on your streets again.' That's when I knew Canada wasn't an English city."

"Were you frightened?" William asked. "When we left Taiwan, I was a bit frightened."

"You were not," Gorrie said, glaring at him. "We were with Mother. Anyway, you were only a baby."

"I know," William said, grinning at her. "But I still wondered if I'd like it."

Tom lowered Betsy's left hind hoof to the ground.

"Well, I was a bit anxious," he admitted, getting to his feet, "but I landed on my feet right enough. Some of the lads were starved worse in Canada than at home and some were expected to do the work of grown men long before they had the strength for it. I ended up with your grandfather though, and he were mortal kind to me. When I'd learned to read, I wanted to put my name in my Bible and I didn't know it. So I asked him if he'd mind my being named Tom Mellis. He said he would count it a compliment and he made it legal. Without people like Dr. Barnardo and your grandpa, I expect I'd have been hanged by now."

"Hanged," Gorrie gasped, her hazel eyes filled with horror.

Tom reached out and ruffled up her dark hair. He gave her an abashed grin.

"Well, maybe not as bad as that," he said. "But I was on my way to becoming a criminal. I stole to eat, you see. And, once you start, it's a slippery slope. I guess you've seen a bit of that from what Mrs. Mellis was after telling me."

"Thanks, Tom," William called as they started for home, leading Betsy.

Gorrie crossed the road with her head down. Had Happy Sid been a boy like Tom? She thought not. He had spoken about his family and, even if some of it had been a lie, she was sure that he had known his parents. What could have gone wrong? She could not understand.

Margaret Ann Gauld was watching for them. As soon as they got to the house, she came out. Tom, who had followed the children to see if he could be of any help, got Betsy between the shafts and hitched her up. Everybody in the family gathered on the verandah to say goodbye as Gret prepared to climb in.

"Can I come?" Gretta asked.

Mother shook her head.

"You'd be wise to take one of the youngsters along," her father advised her in a quiet voice, "You should have company. You might fall asleep on your own and miss the road."

"I doubt I'll be sleepy," said his daughter. Then her glance fell on Gorrie's troubled face. Her own expression softened slightly. "Flora, run and get

your coat. You probably need to clear your con-
science as much as I do."

They jogged along in silence for the first hour.
Gorrie was feeling a bit better by then. It was inter-
esting to journey down an unfamiliar road with
only her mother. The sun shone as though it were
any day. Finally she got up courage enough to ask a
question.

"Why did he do it, Mother? Is he evil? Did he
know, all along, he would rob us?"

Mother shook the reins, encouraging Betsy to
step out a little faster.

"I wouldn't call Mr. Tanner evil exactly," she said
slowly. "I think he was weak. He said he was my
brother Will's friend. Even if he made that up, he
reminded me of Will. Charming, friendly but weak.
Weakness can sometimes cause as much suffering
to others as outright wickedness. You keep hoping
that a weak man will become changed, you see. It
can break the heart, all that hoping and being disappointed. But I believe Sid Tanner wanted to be
the man he pretended to be."

"Oh, he did," Gorrie said. "I know he did."

"How do you know?"

Gorrie told her about the last words Sid had spoken to her.

"Yes," Mother said slowly. "He'd already taken
the key, by then, and he had delivered the mailbag
to the train. So he could not go back. Or he would
have thought it was too late. Try to remember the
man he might have been, Flora, as he asked you to,

and also remember that it is never too late to change your own mind. If you realize you have made a mistake, however hard it may be, admit it and start fresh."

"Did you ever have to do that, Mother?" Gorrie asked in a soft voice.

"Yes," her mother said. "I'm doing it now. Maybe, when I tell the authorities what happened, they will no longer trust me to run the Post Office. It won't be easy to ask them to forgive me."

"No," Gorrie said. She reached over and squeezed her mother's hand. "But I trusted him too."

"You're a child," Margaret Ann Gauld said. "I'm supposed to know better."

Gorrie sat on a straight wooden chair and waited while Mother went into the office. She tried to stop thinking about Sid being arrested and being marched off and locked up in a jail cell. She couldn't. Then she had a sick moment of wondering if the men in the office behind the tall closed door would send her mother to prison. She was crying silently when her mother emerged, her cheeks red, her eyes defiant but a smile on her face for her little girl.

They had supper at an eating house.

"We could have gone to Aunt Nell's, couldn't we?" Gorrie said as Mother ordered meat pies for both of them.

"No," Mother said. "I could confess to the authorities but never, if I can help it, will my in-laws find out."

Gorrie giggled, choking on her first bite of piecrust.

"I have some news for you," Mother said, as they set out again. "I have a feeling it will please you. When we sent word to Wingham of Sid's coming, the police were at the station to meet the train. After they told him they had come to ask him about a mail robbery, he told them his tale about spending the night praying with the murderer and asked if he could be allowed one meal in peace before he went to the police station. He said he felt faint. They took pity on him and let him choose the inn. While they were eating at another table, he went out the back way and escaped. They swear they'll get him yet but I would not be surprised if our Happy Sid gets clean away and is never heard of by that name again."

Gorrie leaned her head against her mother's shoulder and gave a sigh of enormous relief. She didn't have to worry. Sid, with his laughing blue eyes and fair curls, was free.

"Mother," she murmured much later, on the way home, "was he really saved?"

"Only God knows that," Margaret Ann Gauld said gently. Her quiet smile was very like her daughter's.

As Gorrie nodded, on the edge of sleep, she heard her mother beginning to sing softly. She wakened enough to hear the words.

> Lord, Thou hast here Thy ninety and nine,
> Are they not enough for Thee?

But the Shepherd made answer,
This of Mine
Has wandered away from Me:
And, although the road be rough and
steep,
I go to the desert to find My sheep.
I go to the desert to find My sheep.

Gorrie loved that hymn. She struggled to wake up enough to join in. But she could not force her heavy eyelids to lift. Secure in the knowledge that her mother would get the lost lamb all the way to the gates of gold before she stopped singing, Flora Gauld tumbled into deep, untroubled sleep.

8
The Love Light

❖

...First let me hear how the children
Stood round His knee,
And I shall fancy His blessing
Resting on me:
Words full of kindness,
Deeds full of grace,
All in the lovelight
Of Jesus' face.
Frederick Arthur Challinor

Margaret Ann Gauld spent five years in Canada,
raising her children, managing the Post Office and
General Store in place of her blind father and helping her frail but indomitable mother keep house.
She had not regretted her decision at first, but as
time went by, she had known that her husband
missed her sorely. She missed him too. And she
missed the joyous adventure of sharing his work in
the mission field. Kippen, for all its dear familiarity,
lacked challenge. She mulled it over for weeks but,

at last, decided it was time to rejoin Will. After all, she had promised to be his wife "for better, for worse, for richer, for poorer, in sickness and in health, till Death did them part." It was clearly her duty. She did not admit, even to her secret heart, that she was itching to go.

The following night, she waited until everyone had been served and everyone had started to eat. Then she took a deep breath and blurted it out.

"I've decided it is time I went back to Formosa. Your father...Will has been alone long enough."

The faces ringed around the table stared at her in open-mouthed astonishment. She was glad she had told them during the week when Gordon and Harvey were in town attending high school.

"I wrote to Will last night," she gabbled on, doing her best to fill the stricken silence with sound. "And I sent notes to Mime and Lib, asking them to come over for a family conference. We should hear back tomorrow. And I've written to Jen. Everything will be fine, you'll see."

Gorrie had only just turned nine. She tried to take in the meaning of her mother's announcement but could not quite manage it. She'd be seeing Ah Soong again. She tried to recall the face of her beloved amah but it seemed to have fallen out of her memory.

"Eat, Flora. You love mock duck. I got it ready specially," her mother said, her voice unsteady suddenly.

Gorrie smiled at her and took such a big bite she

almost choked. Nobody else seemed to be hungry.

"Your duty is with your husband. I've always felt that," Grandma said. But her words shook a little too. If Grandpa hadn't asked William a riddle, they would all have burst into tears.

When Gordon and Harvey were told the news on Friday evening, they reacted very differently. Gord, about to leave home anyway to attend university, seemed not to mind. He went right on talking about his basketball team winning an important game. But Harvey, when told he would be staying with father's brother in Mimico, went utterly still. And he spent all day Saturday out in the bush somewhere, not even coming in for his dinner at noon.

Then Mother's sisters arrived. Uncle Archie drove Aunt Lib over in time for dinner after church. They were late arriving, of course, and the children were ravenous by the time they took their places. Mother had given them an apple to "stay the pangs" but it had not helped. Will snatched at a piece of bread.

"I must say that children today aren't taught to be as mannerly as we were," Aunt Lib said when William talked with his mouth full.

Seven-year-old William stopped speaking, his exciting story unfinished, his big brown eyes filling with tears.

"I don't think you had to say any such thing, Elizabeth," Grandma said tartly. "I think Gret's children are very polite. They are kind-hearted too, which is more important."

The children gaped at this. She herself so often corrected them sharply. Mother, who had gone red, flashed her a grateful look. William, who had ducked his head to keep his telltale tears from showing, blinked them away and went on eating. None of the other children spoke until the meal was over. Even Dorothy, who was still just four years old and given to happy babbling, looked at Aunt Lib's sour expression and kept mum. The moment they were excused, all the Gauld youngsters ran outside and stayed there.

"Aunt Lib is a grouchy old prune," Gorrie burst out the minute they were out of earshot of the house.

Nobody contradicted her. Dorothy giggled and repeated, to a tune of her own invention, "Grouchy old prune, grouchy old prune." Gretta gave her a quelling glance.

"They can't hear," the little girl said stoutly, "and Gorrie said it first."

"She's so different from the others," Gretta said, relaxing. "I wonder what made her that way."

"Pride," William put in unexpectedly. "I heard Mother tell Grandma once, 'Lib's so top-lofty and proud, she can't enjoy life.'"

Gretta and Gorrie were fascinated.

"What did Grandma say?" they asked with one voice.

"She said, 'Watch that tongue of yours, Gret,'" he quoted, grinning. "'Judge as ye will be judged.'"

They all laughed at his imitation of their grand-mother's tart tone.

"Then she said, 'But I daresay you're right about poor Elizabeth,'" William added.

Uncle Henry brought Aunt Mime from their farm at five o'clock. They had often come for Sunday supper before but this time it felt different. Gorrie and Gretta exchanged puzzled glances. What was wrong with everybody?

As soon as they had finished eating, the two uncles, looking sheepish somehow, took themselves off. Then, even though it wasn't eight o'clock, all the children, including fourteen-year-old Gretta, were sent to bed.

"Why?" Gorrie asked.

"Do as you're told," her mother said, her voice sharp, her eyes worried.

Even Gretta went quietly after that, knowing something was amiss. The minute William and Dorothy had fallen asleep, the older girls knelt down in their room and put their ears to the heat register.

"We can look after ourselves, I tell you. I won't be put out of my own home," they heard Grandma saying. Her voice was shrill and angry.

She's scared, Gorrie thought. But she could not believe her grandmother would be afraid of any-thing.

Finally the girls caught enough bits and pieces to realize that Grandpa and Grandma were being told that they had to go and live with Aunt Lib after the

Gaulds left. Both Gorrie and Gretta were filled with pity. Aunt Lib was the only Mellis sister who seemed never to smile. Whenever she came to visit, their mother was stricter than usual and still Aunt Lib found fault. Once, when she caught Gretta and Gorrie fighting, she made them sit down and memorize a poem which began

> Dogs delight to bark and fight
> For 'tis their nature so...

The whole tone of it made it sound as if Aunt Lib had composed it herself. It went on sternly urging them not to "tear out each other's eyes."

"As if we would," Gorrie had complained to Mother later.

"You can't live alone," Mother was saying to her parents now. She had said these words before, the girls could tell. "We wouldn't have an easy moment. Yet Will needs me to be with him. We've all put you first until now. Now you have to think of us and our families."

She sounded as if she were crying.

Then Grandpa said quietly, "Jane, they've been good and faithful daughters to us all these years. Lib can't leave Archie. The congregation would be scandalized. We'd better go."

"But we've lived in Kippen for fifty years," Grandma wailed.

"It's time we went somewhere else then," Grandpa said gamely. But he sounded very tired.

"He doesn't want to go either," Gorrie whispered.

"Of course he doesn't," Gretta said fiercely, tears in her eyes. "I'm glad Fleet died peacefully here. You know how Aunt Lib feels about dogs."

The next day, the children were told the news and the job of packing began. Closing the Kippen house was harder than Mother's getting herself and her four youngest prepared for going to Aunt Jen's home in Regina. Close to the end, Father came home to help.

There was another painful goodbye scene before they left.

Watching the women's tearful faces, Gorrie wondered who had decided that women had to do all the looking after. Father's sister took care of Grandma Gauld. Maybe Aunt Nell would have liked to go away somewhere. Gorrie knew she would if she were Aunt Nell. Grandma Gauld, like Aunt Lib, seldom smiled. Even Gordon, who dared to tease her a little, was a bit afraid of her.

"Don't worry about them, Gret. You've done your share. If worst comes to worst, I'll go get them," Aunt Mime said quietly. "I'd have taken them to begin with if I didn't have Henry's parents living with me."

"I know," Mother said, keeping her voice down so Aunt Lib would not overhear. "She's just so...so..."

"So very Lib," Aunt Mime half-whispered.

The two women laughed shakily. Gorrie, who

suddenly realized how much she loved her grand-
parents, hoped Aunt Mime would rescue them
from Aunt Lib before long. They looked smaller,
somehow, and more like children. She hugged them
both hard, trying to put all her love for them into
the embrace.

"Goodness, William," Grandma said, doing her
best to ease the parting, "you'll be a young man
when we see you next."

"You won't see him," Dorothy piped up. "You'll
be dead before we come back. Mother said so."

There was a long moment of shocked silence.
Nobody knew what to say.

"The tickets," Father said. "Gret, where did you
put the steamship tickets?"

Everyone hunted high and low. Then, at the last
moment, Father found he had had them in his
breast pocket all along.

"Well done, Will," Gorrie heard her mother murmur mysteriously.

Gorrie got kissed by everyone. Aunt Lib's kiss
was dry and papery. Gorrie watched her give the
other children a peck on the cheek each. They all
shrank back slightly. Gorrie caught a queer look on
her aunt's face as she backed up to stand next to her
husband.

Maybe she's a changeling, Gorrie thought suddenly. She looks lonely.

Then it was time to get into the buggy again and
go to the station. Until the Gaulds were on the train
and headed west, Gorrie took it for granted that she

would be going back to Taiwan with her parents. She guessed that Gretta would have to go to school in Canada like Gord and Harvey. But she never dreamed that her mother would leave her and William behind. After all, she had just turned nine and William was not quite eight. She was not sure when she began to suspect the truth.

"They'll be fine with Jen. Think of how loving she has been to the older boys," she heard her father saying in the berth one night after he thought she was asleep.

"Maybe it's easier for a man," Mother said. "William is still so young and Gorrie is so small."

"You know Gorrie's size does not mean she isn't perfectly healthy. Dr. Tanaka said she might not grow as much as the others and not to let it worry us. And you've had Dr. Cameron look her over here. I know you will miss them. I know that. I'll miss them too, even if I am a man. But..."

Father sounded terribly troubled. Mother was probably crying. He hated it when anyone cried.

Gorrie yawned loudly and thumped over in the bunk above them. The conversation broke off abruptly. There was silence except for the noise of the train. Then her father stood up and peered through the dark green curtains. Gorrie watched him through eyes that looked shut to him but were really open a slit. His head disappeared.

"Why don't we tell them? I have a feeling it's going to be a shock."

"No. I want them to be at Jen's for a day or two

and feel at home there first. Then...perhaps you
could tell them."

"I? Isn't that a mother's job?" Father sounded
agitated.

Gorrie's mother gave a laugh that was rough
with tears.

"I suppose so," she said soothingly. "Remain
calm, William. Of course, I'll do it."

Gorrie dreaded that conversation. One day when
she was mad at Will, she told him what she had
heard. He stared at her and then ran away. He did
not speak to her until the following morning. He
didn't run to ask his parents if it were true. Perhaps
he, too, had already guessed. At last Gorrie, unable
to bear the tension she read in her mother's eyes,
asked Gretta to tell their parents that she and Will
both knew and they didn't want to talk about it.

Gretta did. Gorrie thought her parents would
talk to her anyway but they must have been
relieved. All they said on the subject was, "We are
leaving next Wednesday morning right after breakfast."

All three children looked away. None of them
said a word in answer. None of them could.

As usual, Gretta was already in the kitchen, on the
last morning, being a big help to the grown-ups,
when Gorrie came running down the back stairs.
One glance at Gretta's set face and reddened eyes
told her that her big sister was finding this last
morning as unbearable as she was herself. Still,

trust Gretta Lilias Victoria Gauld to be acting noble about it.

"I'll dish up Gorrie's oatmeal, Mother," Gretta said loudly, rushing over to the big woodstove.

Mother did not answer. She was feeding Dorothy with one hand, even though the little girl had been able to feed herself perfectly well for a couple of years. She had her hat on with the veil thrown back and was wearing her new travelling dress of serviceable navy serge. She looked like a stranger.

"Mother," Gorrie said in a strangled voice. "Mother...where's William?"

"Just three more bites, my baby," Mother said. Then she shot one swift glance at Gorrie.

"Don't call me a baby," Dorothy said indignantly. "I'm four."

Mother ignored this. She answered Gorrie instead.

"William must be still asleep. He might as well go on sleeping till it's closer to the time. He was awake in the night with a bad dream. Thank you, Gretta dear. You're such a help."

Gretta set down the large bowl of oatmeal at Gorrie's place and did her best to smile. Gorrie snatched up the milk jug and splashed too much milk into her bowl. A few drops flew through the air and landed on the table. Dorothy laughed.

"Flora, do be careful," her mother said. She took the napkin she was using to wipe the four-year-old's chin and blotted up the drops.

Gorrie kept her head down. Somebody silently

passed her the sugar bowl. Uncle Jack. She mumbled, "Thank you," without looking at him, sprinkled some sugar onto the oatmeal and dug her spoon into the porridge. At once, the milk rose and threatened to brim over the edge.

Mother did not notice. Gorrie forced herself to take a smaller bite. The porridge, usually so good, tasted flat. Somebody had forgotten to put in the salt.

Gorrie opened her mouth to complain and then thought better of it. Let one of the others get into trouble for criticizing the food. Maybe John or Dave. They belonged here in Regina. She felt as though she did not belong anywhere.

The Balfour kitchen was crowded with people. Aunt Jen was busy making sandwiches for Mother and Father and Dorothy to eat on the train. Dave and John were sitting across from Gorrie. John was eating his porridge as though it tasted fine. Dave was pulling faces at Dorothy, trying to make her giggle. Uncle Jack had risen and gone out into the hall to help Father with the luggage. It was strange how lonesome Gorrie felt with so many people all around her.

Dorothy swallowed her last bite and Mother wiped her mouth. Then the child slid to the floor and made a bee-line for her sister Flora.

"Let me up," she demanded, lapsing into baby-talk.

Gorrie almost burst into tears. Dorothy had on her new dress, also navy serge, with the sailor collar.

Her fair curls shone. She was all ready to go. Father
and Mother were taking her back to Taiwan with
them. She was not old enough to have to stay in
Regina like the other three and attend school. Still,
that was not Dorothy's fault.

Gorrie pushed her chair back and hoisted her little sister's chunky body up onto her lap. Then she
gave her a bear hug. The small girl chortled with
delight.

"Tell me a story about when you were a little
girl," the child commanded.

Gorrie, feeling as though she were still a baby,
gulped hard. In her mind's eye, she saw Ah Soong's
smiling face. Nobody had called her Hoy Bit for
months.

"I'll be back," she had told her beloved amah the
day they had left Taiwan. "Father's work is here."

Now she understood why Ah Soong had turned
away so quickly. She must have guessed that her
parents would not bring her with them when they
returned.

She pushed the little girl away.

"No," she got out. "I don't know any stories."

"Gorrie has to eat her breakfast," her mother
explained, looking into Dorothy's surprised face
with such a loving look that Gorrie felt suddenly
heartsick. It was like the hymn they had sung last
night at bedtime, "Tell Me the Stories of Jesus."

> Words full of kindness,
> deeds full of grace,

All in the lovelight of Jesus' face.

That was how Mother looked, as though her face, too, held the lovelight.

"Gorrie, Adam and Eve and Pinch Me went down to the river to swim," Dave said, from across the table. "If Adam and Eve were drowned, who was saved?"

Gorrie looked at him with scorn. She had known that one for years. Her big brother Gordon, now eighteen and starting university, had tricked her with it when she was William's age.

"If you aren't going to eat your porridge, Flora," her mother said, "you might as well go and get William up. We'll be leaving for the station in less than an hour. Don't upset him, mind. Just help him dress and bring him down."

Gorrie slipped out of her chair, thankful to escape. As she rounded the table, she reached out with lightning swiftness and tweaked Dave's ear.

"Pinch you," she sang out.

"Flora Gauld, what on earth…" Aunt Jen sounded shocked.

Gorrie did not stop to defend herself. She flew up the stairs two steps at a time to waken her little brother. He was sharing a room with the older boys.

He should be able to get dressed by himself but he was given to dreaming and it took him forever. Also he still was not good at tying shoes and parting his hair and buttoning his shirt straight.

"Wake up," she said, pushing open the bedroom

door.

But the bed was empty. Her eyes flew to the chair where she and Gretta had laid out his clothes for this morning when they helped get him ready for bed the night before. The chair was empty too. William had gotten up and dressed without any help and had vanished.

Filled with sudden excitement which helped to ease the ache in her heart, she went pounding down to the kitchen again.

"He's not there," she announced. "William's not there. And his clothes are gone. He got himself up."

Gretta did not believe her, of course. She ran up to check. But when she returned, wide-eyed, to report that her sister had been telling the truth, everyone began to hunt frantically for the small boy.

He was nowhere to be found.

"We'll have to go," Father said, "or we'll miss the train."

"But, Will," Mother cried and then stopped.

Would she have cried out like that if I'd been missing? Gorrie wondered.

They bundled into Uncle Jack's newfangled car—Mother, Father, Dorothy, Gretta and Gorrie and the pile of suitcases. Where they would have put William she could not imagine. Aunt Jen stayed behind with her two boys.

"I'll take good care of them, Gret," she promised. "I'll write regularly to give you news. You take care of yourselves. God bless you."

She was weeping and had to hush. John and Dave were staring at her, their eyes wide with alarm. Mother was crying too and the baby was thinking of joining in.

Uncle Jack did not wait. He cranked up the engine and leaped into the car as soon as it coughed into life. They were off!

Then Gorrie saw her little brother. He was sitting on a fence, watching for the car to go by.

"There's William," she said, pointing.

"William!" Mother cried out, struggling to open the car window.

"We can't stop," Father said. He sounded hoarse. "We'll be late if we stop."

Mother was waving frantically. Gorrie stared up into her face. If only, just once, Mother would look at her that way!

William watched them. He did not wave. He looked terribly small and alone. Gorrie felt a great sob pushing up out of her throat. She swallowed hard. She hated crying in public. Father was not crying. He would want her to be brave.

She remembered the Bible verse she had found in church last Sunday: "When my father and my mother forsake me, then the Lord will take me up."

I hate the Lord, she thought. It was the Lord who was calling Father to go back to help preach the gospel to the people in Taiwan. They did not know that Jesus loved them, he had explained. Gorrie knew someone should go and tell them but she did not understand why it had to be Father who did it.

Gretta felt the same way, she was sure, although they both knew better than to speak their heretical thoughts aloud.

The car stopped with a jerk. The train was coming. They could hear its whistle and the hum of its wheels on the track. Gretta scrambled out onto the platform and Gorrie followed after her. There seemed to be a lot of people moving about, kissing each other.

Mother bent and kissed Gorrie fast. She did not look at her, not really. She seemed like a stranger again. Her face was stiff behind the dotted veil of her hat and her mouth was twisting.

"Mother," Gretta sobbed, throwing herself at their mother.

"I know you'll be a brave girl, my Gretta, and help Aunt Jen all you can. Remember that you are fourteen now, almost a woman," Mother said.

"We must get on the train," Father told her. "God bless you, Flora."

The words sounded formal and hurried. Gorrie felt forgotten, abandoned. Not helpful like Gretta. Not small like William.

Then a big arm came around her shoulders. She looked up, astonished, into her Uncle Jack's face. He said nothing but his hug said that she mattered to him. She was not all alone.

"Goodbye," she called, breaking free and running to wave at her parents framed in the grimy train window.

Dorothy had begun to bellow.

Mother waved. She looked straight at Gorrie. Her lips moved.

Gorrie couldn't hear the words because of the train whistle but she knew what her mother had said.

"Take care of William, Flora."

Not Gretta. Mother wanted her, Gorrie, to do this.

"I will," she called as the train began to move. "I promise."

Then the three of them, Gretta crying so hard she had the hiccoughs, Uncle Jack blowing his nose like a trumpet and Gorrie, were left. They stood bunched together on the platform, watching the train growing smaller and, at last, disappearing altogether.

"Let's go home," Flora Gauld said. "William will be lonely."

9
The Stormy Blast

O God, our help in ages past,
Our hope for years to come,
Our shelter in the stormy blast,
And our eternal home.
ascribed to William Croft

Despite Uncle Jack's hug and Mother's asking her to look after William, Gorrie found the weeks after her parents left for Taiwan flat and unreal. Even with a new city to explore, a new school to find her way in and the Balfours to get used to, she felt adrift and alone. Then, in June, the cyclone hit Regina.

It wasn't until the family were on their way home from church that they felt the wind strengthening alarmingly. One powerful gust snatched off Gretta's new hat and sent it bowling along the sidewalk.

133

"My hat!" she shrieked and went chasing down
Spruce Street after it. She would not have caught up
with it if it had not snagged on a prickly bush. The
other children cheered as she waved it triumphant-
ly above her head. Her hair, which had taken her
ages to pin up, tumbled down. It blew straight up
and then, as another gust snatched at it, whipped
frontwards, hiding her face entirely.

Gorrie, helpless with laughter, felt her own hat
tugging to get away and clutched at it, thankful, for
the first time in her life, for the elastic which cut
into the soft skin under her chin.

When they dashed into the house, nobody but
Aunt Jen gave a thought to lunch. The moment
their hats and gloves and hymnbooks were
dropped on the hall table, all the children joined
Uncle Jack on the upstairs verandah.

"Hail!" John shouted, turning up his face

The boys pelted back down the stairs and rushed
out trying to see who could get the biggest hail-
stone. Gorrie dashed after them and began to
snatch the icy pellets up too.

"I've got one the size of a golfball," her cousin
Dave yelled.

"Mine's as big as an egg," his brother John called
back.

"Mine's as big as…as big as a baseball," shrieked
William.

Gorrie knew he was lying but she looked anyway. He had raced out into the deluge and run right
back again, empty-handed, when the hailstones

stung his upturned face. But he was jumping up and down and making as much noise as any of the older kids.

"Flora, boys, come back here. You, too, Gretta," Uncle Jack called down to them, using his hands as a megaphone. "Be quick. I want you to look at a cloud."

The neighbours were out on their verandahs too, all staring in the same direction. As Gorrie reached her uncle's side, she heard a man's voice call out, "It's a cyclone! It's heading straight for us."

"He's from the States," Uncle Jack laughed, "where they have such things."

Gorrie stared, wide-eyed, at the strange greenish funnel of cloud twisting through the sky. It seemed to lift and then touch down again.

"Jack, it's hit Germantown," someone else called. "They're going to be wiped out."

The trees along the street were bent nearly double and their limbs were thrashing wildly, straining to go with the gale. Smaller branches and twigs tore free and flew through the air. Aunt Jen, looking pale with shock, had joined them.

"Jack, it's a real twister," Gorrie heard her say. "Jim's house… It's near Jim's house."

Then the writhing cloud snaked past and was gone. Uncle Jack turned and ran into the house.

"What are you going to do?" Aunt Jen called.

"I'm going to drive over there and see," they heard him shout.

Everyone stood stock-still, staring. Uncle Jack

never, ever drove his car on Sunday. He was not a
man who broke his own rules. But Uncle Jim was
his brother.

"Wait, Dad," John called down then, racing for
the stairs. "I want to come too."

He might not have taken them if he had not had
to crank the engine to get it going. By the time it
had roared into life, all five children had piled into
the Ford.

"Jack, this is crazy," Aunt Jen said to him as he
sprang to get in. "There's broken glass everywhere.
The tires will be cut to ribbons."

He looked at her through the window, his face
grim.

"I have to try," he said. "If we get a flat, we'll
walk from there."

"Squeeze over, children," Aunt Jen rapped out.
"You're not leaving me here alone to worry myself
sick. Stop squealing, William, and sit on your sister's lap. There's plenty of room."

Everyone laughed crazily at that. They were
jammed in tighter than sardines in a can. The car
seemed to creep along although really Gorrie's
uncle drove as fast as he could. As they neared
Uncle Jim's house, they saw a whole tree uprooted,
a big armchair, a bucket caught upside down on a
hitching post, a stove in the middle of the road and
a car twisted as if some giant had taken it in his
great hands and bent it out of shape. They could
hear people screaming. Then, without a single
puncture, they were at Uncle Jim's.

The children were to remember the next few moments all their lives. The family was alive. Everyone was shaken and bruised but no bones had been broken. But the roof was gone and it looked as though someone had taken a huge spoon and stirred up everything in the house. Every window was shattered. The pictures were off the walls. All the cupboard doors swung open and there was broken glass everywhere. Aunt Aggie was sitting on the one kitchen chair still right side up and moaning softly.

"Thank God you're alive," Aunt Jen said. She set another chair on its legs and sat down next to her sister-in-law. "Aggie, Aggie, it's over and you're all safe."

"I'll never feel safe again," Aunt Aggie whimpered and Aunt Jen hugged her as though she were William's size.

Gorrie watched, wondering where Uncle Jim's family would sleep. That morning, in church, they had sung "O God, our help in ages past..." She remembered the lines, "Our shelter in the stormy blast/ And our eternal home." If God was really their shelter in the stormy blast, He had not done a very good job of it. Gorrie had been upstairs. You could stand in the front bedroom and look straight up into the sky. Where would they sleep? If it rained in the night, they'd be soaked.

"You're coming home with us," Aunt Jen said firmly. "You needn't even pack. We're close to the same size and Jack can supply Jim's needs. We have plenty of children's things. Aggie, were the little ones very frightened?"

Aunt Aggie sniffed and then gave a shaky laugh.

"I had all I could do to keep hold of them," she said. "They were for chasing outside. If I hadn't kept a good grip on them, they'd have blown away with the roof and landed somewhere in Manitoba, like as not."

Gorrie blinked. A moment before, Aunt Aggie had been trembling in fear; now she was laughing. Was this God working or just Aunt Jen? She didn't know but she had a funny feeling it came to the same thing.

"Gorrie, come and see," William shrieked, dashing into the room and out again.

"See what?" she called, tearing after him.

It was the roof. It was sitting, almost all in one piece, on top of a shed two backyards down the street. Gorrie stared at it and felt slightly queasy. Until that moment, houses had felt solid and durable. She had heard adults say, "It's as safe as houses." She knew new homes were built and, occasionally, old ones were demolished. But she had never imagined they could come apart like this, without help from anything but a wind. It was exciting and terrifying at one and the same time.

"It shouldn't take too long to get that back in place," Uncle Jack said, peering up at the roof.

"It'll take long enough," his brother said morosely.

"Everyone will help," Uncle Jack said. "And you

can stay with us, of course."

Where would they sleep? Gorrie knew where. At least one of the girls would be put in with her and Gretta. She sighed. It was hard now to find secret places in which to read for hours. With these visitors, it would be impossible.

"They're all coming to our house to stay," she told Gretta.

"I knew they would," Gretta said.

Gorrie looked up at the cloudy sky, now letting watery sunshine through.

"O God, our help in ages past," she said softly, "try not to need our 'shelter' for too long. Gretta's and my bed feels pretty crowded already."

She did not know Aunt Jen had come out and was watching her until she spoke.

"Flora, what are you thinking about staring up into space like that? You look half-witted," she said, her own anxiety about the days to come sharpening her voice.

Gorrie jerked her gaze down to her aunt's worried face and told the truth.

"I was praying."

Aunt Jen's face softened at once.

"Good for you, honey," she said. "We're going to need His help in the next few days. Round up William. I have to go home and start getting things ready."

Running after her little brother, who had chosen this moment to vanish, Gorrie found herself thinking of the Prodigal Son. She had never liked him much. But now, for the first time in her life, she wondered if they had had enough beds back then. Maybe the Elder Brother was such a grouch because he knew he'd have to put up with the younger one's sharing his bed, grinding his teeth maybe, or snoring. William ground his teeth every night.

Then she caught her brother and forgot hymns and parables. As Aunt Jen had said, there was a lot of work waiting. She wasn't going to have enough time to herself. Thank goodness Gretta never seemed to mind doing dishes or even dusting.

For the children, the next three weeks flew by. School was cancelled while Regina recovered. The adults, even those who were as a rule not friendly, talked and talked about how shocking the cyclone was and what damage they or their relations had suffered. The church collected money to help out the people in Germantown. The minister preached about feeding the hungry and healing the sick and visiting the lonely. They sang "Rock of Ages" with new gusto and then "O God Our Help in Ages Past." Gorrie sent a secret smile to God.

One night, after Uncle Jim's family had finally gone home and she and Gretta were at the kitchen table doing their homework, Gorrie looked up from her arithmetic problems and said, "I wonder if Mother has our letters about the cyclone yet."

Gretta was silent. Gorrie caught a funny look on her face.

"What's wrong?" she asked.

"In Taiwan, they have earthquakes and

typhoons," her sister said at last. "I was wondering
about them too. It just takes so long for news to
come. I almost wish we hadn't told them."

Gorrie looked troubled for a second. Then her
face cleared.

"If we hadn't, somebody else would have," she
said. "They won't believe it was as bad as it was.
And we're all perfectly safe. Uncle Jim even has his
roof back on. Did you read what William wrote?"

Gretta chuckled.

"Yes," she said. "'Hailstones as big as baseballs.'
Even Father will have to laugh at that."

Five minutes later, they both appeared to be
hard at work again. But, in reality, Gorrie was writing to Mother telling her not to worry and Gretta
was scrawling a note to Father begging him to send
a reassuring cable in the event of a severe earth-
quake or typhoon. Taiwan was so far away. Home
for Gretta and Gorrie was here in Regina now. But
Mother and Father and Dorothy were still their
family.

When the two of them asked Aunt Jen for a
stamp, she laughed and put their letters into an
envelope which already contained a letter she herself had written.

"It's a good thing I hadn't sealed it yet," she said.
"I wrote to tell your mother what good sports you
were when the house was so crowded and there
was so much extra work to be done. I may not have
a daughter of my own but you two have shown me
how lovely it is to have girls in the family. There.

It's ready to mail. Why don't you both run to the post-box with it?"

"How did she guess we wanted to mail it tonight?" Gorrie marvelled as the flap on the post-box banged down.

"Mothers just know," Gretta said. "I guess aunts do too."

10
O Valiant Hearts

…Bring me my bow of burning gold!
Bring me my arrows of desire!
Bring me my spear! Oh clouds, unfold!
Bring me my chariot of fire!

I will not cease from mental fight,
Nor let my sword sleep in my hand,
Till we have built Jerusalem
In England's green and pleasant land.

William Blake

"One, two, buckle my shoe," Gorrie chanted as she skipped. "Three, four, shut the door."

She was free. All her friends were working away in a stuffy classroom, but she had got off school because of her dental appointment. When she was eleven, Uncle Jack and Aunt Jen had decided to have her teeth straightened. It was a brand new thing and her crooked, crowded teeth were just what the dentist wanted to experiment on. Because she had had nephritis they had grown in overlapping. The rest of the family had beautiful teeth and she envied them. But they didn't get out of school regularly, as she did, to get their braces adjusted.

She took her skipping rope and skipped right across Victoria Park to the dentist's office, pretending she was Mary Lennox skipping down the long walk at Misselthwaite Manor. Even though she had loved all the Anne of Green Gables stories she had read, her favourite book was still *The Secret Garden*. She had been given it the Christmas before she turned ten and she had spent all Christmas afternoon lying on her bed reading it. They had called to her to come out for a walk but she had not answered. She was already out in the hidden garden with Dickon and Colin. Who would come back to ordinary old Regina from Misselthwaite Manor?

"You should read it, Aunt Jen," she said. "I know you'd love it."

The next day, when the children came home for lunch, they caught Aunt Jen deep in the book, completely unaware of the time.

"Moses and Aaron, it can't be that late!" she exclaimed, jumping up and rushing to put on the kettle.

Gorrie grinned at her. She was glad to have given her hard-working aunt a trip to the moors, where she could smell the heather and listen to the larks singing.

Not long after Gorrie began to have her teeth straightened, a nurse tested the eyesight of all the children at school.

"Are you sure you can't read the next line?" she asked, as though Gorrie was mixing up the letters on purpose.

Gorrie squinched up her eyes and tried again. The nurse clucked her tongue disapprovingly and sent Flora Gauld home with a note telling her aunt she should have her vision checked.

"You must have been having trouble at school," the eye doctor said. "You are decidedly myopic."

"What does myopic mean?" Gorrie asked.

"Short-sighted," the doctor said.

Gorrie did not realize, until she got glasses, what an enormous difference they would make in her life. She stared through them at the blackboard. The fuzzy chalk marks of yesterday were sharp and clear now. And faces she had believed herself to be seeing were suddenly filled with beloved details she had lost so gradually she had not known they were gone.

"You don't look like Gorrie in those," William said.

"I don't care," Gorrie said. "You look more like William than you have in ages."

She lay in bed at night thinking about her parents, trying to bring their faces clearly into focus the way she had William's. She saw them as they looked in familiar photographs but it was difficult now to remember them properly as she had last seen them. She felt sad because she did not miss them as much as she should and she loved Aunt Jen and Uncle Jack so much. She made herself be careful as she wrote letters to Tamsui not to sound quite as happy as she really was.

Gorrie turned twelve in 1914. Gretta was finishing high school, managing to pass her exams without too much difficulty. They had a happy spring and spent their usual family summer holiday at Regina Beach. All winter, they dreamed about the two weeks they spent camping by the lake. Each family group slept separately in a tent or cabin but they all ate together in the huge dining tent. They had campfires when it got dark and sang "Danny Boy" and "There's a Long, Long Trail A-winding" and "Clementine" and "Funiculi, Funicula."

It meant hard work for the women but for the men and children it was a short stay in paradise. And the women enjoyed it too, even though they complained a bit. It was such a change having other women to share in each day's chores and challenges.

One evening the whole family was playing baseball. They had put Gorrie out in the field and she was wondering if she could pick up *Chronicles of Avonlea* off the grass beside her foot and read a little without anyone noticing when she heard Dave shrieking, "The ball! Get it, Gorrie! Catch it!"

Nobody thought she really would. She knew that perfectly well as she ran backwards staring up at the descending fly ball. Up went her two hands. Whap! She sat down on the grass, clutching the softball to her chest. Then she looked across the length of the baseball diamond at her uncle. He waved to her and handed the bat to William. She had actually got Uncle Jack out by catching his long high fly ball. Her marvellous deed ended the inning and her side came to bat.

"When you caught that ball, Gorrie," Dave said after the game was over, "I was so astounded I almost fainted dead away."

Gorrie knew that, although his words sounded insulting, he meant them as a compliment. She grinned back at him.

"I was pretty astounded myself," she admitted. "I'd stopped paying attention. If you hadn't yelled at me, I'd not even have seen it coming let alone caught it."

"Dad was surprised too, I can tell you," Dave said. "I heard him telling Mother. 'I was proud of her. She kept her eye on the ball and, once she had it, she held onto it,' he said."

Gorrie was so pleased she did not know what to do with her exuberant joy. Needing an outlet, she punched Dave between the shoulder-blades. He whirled on her, laughing aloud, and buffeted her in return. William, who was becoming quieter as he grew older, stood watching with a little grin.

"David Balfour, you must never hit a girl," Aunt Jen said.

They had not known she was watching. Gorrie opened her mouth to say she had started it when she saw her aunt was smiling.

"Don't worry, Mother. I'll never hit a girl again—unless she hits me first," Dave promised.

None of them knew that an archduke had been assassinated that day in far away Sarajevo. If they had been aware of it, the young people would have seen no connection between the fact and their lives. It was so distant, so unreal.

But the following afternoon, Uncle Jack studied the *Leader Post* with a grim expression.

"What is it, Jack?" Aunt Jen asked, her attention caught by the strain she saw in his face.

"Trouble in the Balkans. I hope it doesn't blow up into something serious," he answered. "These headlines are irresponsible, in my opinion. If there's going to be a war, boys like Gordon may get swept off their feet..."

"Oh, no, Jack, they have too much sense," Aunt Jen assured him, turning back to gathering up the supper dishes. "It has nothing to do with us. Come on, Flora. Put down that book and pick up a dish-towel."

Gorrie laid down Anne Shirley's story with a sigh. If only Uncle Jack had gone on talking about the news for two more minutes, she might have escaped. Then Gretta would have pitched in and taken her place. After all, Gretta loved doing dishes.

Aunt Jen was wrong: the war came, and Canada joined the fight against Germany. Gordon did not rush to enlist, however. And with the new songs everyone began singing, like "Pack Up Your

Troubles in Your Old Kit Bag" and "It's a Long Way to Tipperary," Gorrie found the war more exciting than frightening.

Then, in May of 1915, eight months after the Great War had begun, when Gorrie was thirteen years old, a ship called the *Lusitania* was sunk by the Germans. It was not a troop ship. Many women and children died in the icy waters of the Atlantic. Uncle Jack, reading the huge headlines, muttered, "This will do it."

"Do what?" Gretta asked.

"If I don't miss my guess," he said, "this will send your brothers to enlist."

He was right. The word came by letter three days later. Gord was in the army and hoping to get into the air corps when it became a reality. He had done his best to talk his younger brother out of following his example but Harvey had insisted on signing up too. Gordon had completed his BA and had planned to go into law. Harvey had only just finished his first year in medical school.

"What a waste!" Aunt Jen wept.

"They had to go. I'd go myself if they'd take me," Uncle Jack told her.

"Don't you dare, Jack Balfour!" his wife flashed back. "As if I could manage this household without your help."

"I wish we could see them in uniform," a neighbour said. "Gordon especially has always been such a handsome lad."

"What a fool that woman is!" Aunt Jen snapped

the minute she was out of hearing. Then her eyes filled with tears. "We must pray to God to watch over them both," she finished.

"I'm going too, Mother," John said.

"You are going upstairs to do your homework, young man," his mother retorted. "You are far too young to think of enlisting."

The next day everyone was down in the dumps. They sat in church listening to a sermon about "our brave boys overseas." They sang "Onward, Christian Soldiers" and "Fight the Good Fight." They were walking home in glum silence when Aunt Jen exclaimed, "Flora Gauld, you didn't darn that stocking. I can see a great hole in the heel from here."

Gorrie swung around to face her, put her nose in the air and recited in her most dramatic voice:

Two men looked out
through the prison bars.
The one saw mud...
the other stars!

Aunt Jen laughed in spite of herself. Uncle Jack let out a whoop they could have heard a block away. Gorrie faced front again, delighted to have cheered them up.

Gorrie completed her four years in high school when she was fifteen. Aunt Jen was concerned about her reading so much.

"Your uncle and I have decided to keep you out of school next year," she said one night. "You can help me with the housework. There is a lot for you to learn before you have a home of your own."

She wrote to Flora's parents in Taiwan.

Mother's letter, reaching them a month later, sounded decidedly skeptical.

"Unless Flora has changed beyond recognition, she'll have her nose in a book whenever she's not under your eye," she commented. "But do what you think best."

Gorrie would have been outraged if it had not been so true. As it was, she gave a guilty laugh and felt closer to her mother than she had in months. Even far away in Taiwan, Mother knew her daughter very well indeed.

"Well, really!" Aunt Jen said, sounding annoyed.

Yet Gorrie saw the twinkle in her eye.

Gorrie had to read. She had started on the family set of books by Charles Dickens and Sir Walter Scott. She would escape from the kitchen, climb a tree and, hidden in its leafy branches, lose herself in *David Copperfield* or *Ivanhoe*. None of the pimply boys she knew at school were half as exciting as the heroes of the novels she devoured, one after another.

Then Gorrie's world changed again: Dad and Mother sent Dorothy home. She was ten now, and her parents wanted her to go to school in Canada. Miss Campbell, a maiden lady of good reputation, was going to Canada on furlough and agreed to take charge of the child. She had not spent much time with children and had never before been in full charge of one. She eyed the sulky youngster with profound misgiving. Then she made up her mind to see what some no-nonsense discipline could accomplish.

Right up to the moment of departure, Dorothy kept begging to stay with her mother. The scene on the wharf was painful for all three Gaulds. Miss Campbell thought they were letting the child make a spectacle of herself.

"Come along," she said sternly. "Let's have no more tears. You're worse than a watering can."

It was not a pleasant voyage for either of them. Miss Campbell found other adults on board to sympathize with her. Dorothy Gauld found nobody and felt utterly forsaken in a cold, hard world. By the time they neared Regina, they were travelling mostly in a hostile silence.

Yet much as the ten-year-old longed to escape from her keeper, she dreaded meeting the hordes of unknown relatives who would be lined up at the station. They would probably disapprove of her as much as Miss Campbell had done. Head down, heart hammering, she followed the woman down the steep steps to the station platform where Gorrie, six years before, had said goodbye to her parents.

"Dorothy, here are your family," Miss Campbell said in her bracing voice.

Dorothy's chin came up. Then, to her enormous relief, she saw a face she remembered. Gorrie was older now but the child remembered sitting on her knee while her beloved big sister told her stories or bounced her up and down and chanted "Hey diddle diddle."

Dorothy's tense little face lit up with blazing joy. She ran to her older sister and clutched her in a fierce hug.

"You're Flora," she sobbed. "I remember you."

Gretta, who was now teaching in a one-room schoolhouse in a town near Regina and had come home especially to meet Dorothy, was miffed.

"How about me? Don't you remember me?" she demanded.

Dorothy raised her tear-wet face from Gorrie's shoulder.

"Are you Gretta?" she asked. "You must be. I know you from pictures. But I don't remember anyone but Flora."

"Never mind," Aunt Jen said, patting the small, stiff back. "You'll know us all soon enough."

That night, Dorothy insisted on sleeping with Gorrie. Gretta stalked off to the spare room where she could have a bed to herself. Desperately homesick, the little girl poured out all her grief and her grievances.

"I don't see why I had to come here," she sobbed. "I can read perfectly well and Father taught me arithmetic. I begged them to let me stay in Taiwan and Mother would have if it weren't for Father. I heard them going over it lots of times."

"You mean you eavesdropped," Gorrie said in a

shocked voice, conveniently forgetting all the times she had listened in on adults.

"I had to," Dorothy said defiantly. "He kept saying, 'Think of the child, Gret. We must let her go for her own good.' And Mother would cry and cry. I don't know how he could be so cruel."

Gorrie, listening to the long tale of woe, saw clearly what her father had been up against. Dorothy did need to be with other children. She just wished Aunt Jen and Uncle Jack were not about to send her away again. She could not tell her little sister the plan they had made, not on the first night. Morning would be time enough.

They told her at breakfast.

"Well, Dorothy," Aunt Jen said in an overly cheery voice, "we've made a plan for you which I'm certain you'll like."

Gorrie braced herself for another flood of tears. Her aunt and uncle had decided that Gretta should take Dorothy to live with her in the home where she boarded. That way, they would have each other and neither would be so alone.

Aunt Jen had taken in her sister's children, first Gordon and Harvey, then Gretta, Gorrie and William. She had her own two boys to care for and, every so often, a niece or nephew of Uncle Jack's would live with them while going to high school in Regina. So many young people living under her roof had both kept her young and worn her out. She would have taken Dorothy in too but Uncle Jack had put his foot down with surprising firmness.

"You've done enough for Gret's children," he had said. "You need a rest. Gretta can care for her sister. She'll make the child welcome. You've taught her how it's done."

"I don't want to leave Flora," Dorothy said piteously.

Gorrie wished Gretta had not heard that. But there was nothing she could do to help. With two other sisters, the plan might have been the best thing that could have happened.

But Gretta was prickly, easily hurt. She hated teaching. And it was plain to Gorrie, from the start, that Dorothy was unhappy.

"Spoiled," Gretta would soon say, agreeing with Miss Campbell and forgetting her own misery at first being separated from her indulgent mother.

Gorrie could not argue with that. It was clearly all too true. Being the only child in a mission compound would have made Dorothy precious to everyone. Mother had found it hard to let her last chick go and had made a baby of her.

"It isn't her fault," Gorrie was to insist over and over again.

When Dorothy confided that she hated her first name, everyone but Gorrie laughed. Gorrie, remembering how much names mattered, called her "Betty" until she was grown-up enough to like the name Dorothy.

"She wets the bed," Gretta said, furious at having to wash bedsheets for a ten-year-old.

"Not because she wants to, Gretta. Get a cot for

her. She's so homesick," Gorrie suggested.

"Easy for you to talk," Gretta snorted. But she did get Dorothy a separate cot.

The war had now lasted two and a half years. Many men who had gone away bravely and even blithely had returned shell-shocked or missing a limb. Gorrie found the war becoming unbearably real as she went to the hospital to help cheer "the wounded heroes" who had been shipped home to Regina. As a small girl, she had played a game called Shipwreck while she washed dishes. The plates and cutlery and glasses had been saved from death by drowning and nursed back to new life. It had seemed so simple then.

Now she was haunted by the suffering she beheld. She lost weight. She began to have trouble sleeping and even the novels she read could not hold her attention as they once had.

One night, after she went with her Sunday School teacher and two other girls to sing to the men in the wards, she came home chuckling.

"That's better," Aunt Jen said. "I've hated your going since I know it's given you sleepless nights. What happened tonight?"

Gorrie helped herself to a handful of oatmeal cookies and slumped wearily in a kitchen chair.

"We sang and sang and nobody cared," she said with her mouth full. "Then Miss Maynard said we would just sing one more. She was strumming away on her autoharp and we were singing and nobody even smiled. Then we sang the line, 'And lose yourself in heaven above.' One big man at the end of the ward waved his crutch in the air and yelled out, 'Sing on! Sing on, girls. You couldn't lose yourselves in a better place.'"

Aunt Jen poured herself and her niece a cup of tea. She laughed.

"Then what happened?"

"Well, it was funny. When he shouted, we all at once became visible. Everyone began to smile and two of them sang along. Before long, they were almost all singing. And they wouldn't let us go for ages."

Harvey and Gordon had both served in the trenches before they volunteered for the Royal Air Corps. Both were accepted but Harvey stayed in Belgium while Gordon returned to England. Harvey was in Flanders for months, and from there he wrote Gorrie the only letter she ever got from him.

> Don't believe what they tell you. I
> shouldn't tell you but I have to tell
> someone. I saw two of my friends
> killed today. They were bleeding to
> death in the mud and I could do noth-
> ing. I think I'll hear their screams all
> my life. Don't believe war is glorious. It
> is too terrible to be borne. I dreamed
> last night that I was skating with you
> on a river somewhere in the moonlight.

> When I woke to the deafening noise of
> the guns, I cried…

Gorrie cried too. Then she hid the two crumpled pages in her Bible. She kept the letter secret, knowing he had written it to her because he had to tell someone but did not think it right to spill it out to Aunt Jen.

A much happier letter came from Gordon the next week. He was in love with Marjorie White, that was clear. He wrote about her for two and a half pages. Then he went on to tell them he was safe in a green and pleasant land. They all knew that he meant England. It was in Blake's poem about the New Jerusalem.

He said he was sure the war was coming to an end.

> Don't worry about me, darling Aunt
> Jen. I've had too many narrow escapes
> to get killed now. In no time, I'll be
> home for one of our talks together. In
> the meantime, I travel around this
> country every chance I get. It really is
> "green and pleasant." If I was not so
> proud of being a Canadian, I might set-
> tle here after the war…

They read it and were comforted, not knowing until later that by the time they got his letter, his plane had been sabotaged and exploded in mid-air.

It had plummeted to earth, killing both the student pilot and Gordon, his teacher.

So Gorrie's big brother stayed in a serviceman's grave "in England's green and pleasant land." He was awarded a medal for his bravery, a Distinguished Flying Cross. It was not much of a consolation.

As the war moved toward its end, the Gaulds and Balfours had trouble rejoicing. Harvey would be coming home any day but Gordon, the shining star of the family, would never know the battle had ended.

Mother and Father were coming home that summer of 1918. The seven of them would all live together in Toronto where the five remaining Gauld children could go on with their education. Maybe healing would come to them there.

But Flora Gauld had not seen her parents for seven years. While she was excited at the prospect of being with them, she was also saddened at leaving Aunt Jen who, if truth were told, she felt closer to than she did to her mother.

One day she was playing basketball when her glasses flew off. Before she could recover her footing, she stepped hard on them, breaking both lenses. Now there would have to be new glasses. Gorrie hated asking for new ones but she could not manage without them.

"Aunt Jen, my glasses broke," she said, staring at the floor, "and I think I need a new prescription."

"Whatever you need, Flora, you shall have," her

aunt said gently. "Don't look so tragic. The money for a pair of glasses is neither here nor there."

They went to the optometrist's, where Gorrie gazed longingly at the pinces-nez. They were completely impractical. Her father would think them frivolous. Aunt Jen saw that look. Aunt Jen always saw.

"We'll take these," she told the man, sounding reckless. "We need to be foolish."

Gorrie Gauld sailed out of the office with the nonsensical glasses perched insecurely on her nose. A brisk wind blew them off at once and she was grateful for the black satin ribbon, which had looked foolish dangling there but kept them from falling to the cement sidewalk and breaking before she'd had them an hour.

The wind was a warm wind, telling of spring. The storm of war in Europe was almost over. She had turned sixteen. At last, her foolish new glasses seemed to say, the time for the singing of the birds had come.

"Oh, Aunt Jen," Gorrie burst out, "I do love you."

"I know," said the woman at her side. "I know, Flora. We love you too."

They walked on to the bus stop together without another word. No words were needed.

11
Velut Arbor Aevo

...Who so beset him round
With fearful stories
Do but themselves confound:
His strength the more is.
No lion can him fright.
He'll with a giant fight,
But he will have the right
To be a pilgrim.

John Bunyan

"Today! They're coming today!" Dorothy shrieked.

Gorrie gave a loud moan.

"What did I ever do to deserve such a noisy sister?" she demanded of heaven.

Dorothy giggled.

"You can't fool me," she said, bouncing up and down on the bed. "You're as excited as I am."

"I don't think it's possible for anyone but Betty

161

Gauld to be that excited," said Gorrie, using the pet name her sister loved. "We'd better get up before you explode."

As she put on her clothes and advised Dorothy about hers, she thought about Dorothy's claim that their excitement was the same. She was eager to see her parents, of course, after the long separation. But, if truth were told, she was also nervous about the meeting. She was no longer little Flora Millicent Gauld, the shy nine-year-old to whom her mother and father had waved goodbye. She had grown up. She had changed. Had they?

She was pensive throughout breakfast. William was too. He had confided to her that he hardly remembered their father.

"Will he want me to be like Gordon?" he had asked uneasily.

"No," Gorrie had reassured him. "He'll want you to be like William. I believe you and he are very alike, now I come to think about it."

The train was due just before lunch. The children went to the station in one big group. Only Harvey was missing. He had been demobilized but was still not home. Every day they waited for news of him.

When William and Margaret Ann Gauld appeared at the door of the train, Dorothy did not wait for the step to be lowered before she flung herself at them. Her father caught and lifted her to safety. As he stepped down to the platform, Dorothy wept like a salty fountain, dampening his coat thoroughly and half-strangling him with her thin arms.

"Come, come, dear child," he said gently at last, "moderate your transports."

Gorrie's heart lifted at the familiar words. Gretta then followed her younger sister's example, except her tears were mixed with laughter. Seeing Mother hugging Gretta, Gorrie reached for William's hand and moved to take Dorothy's place.

"Let go, Betty," she said, detaching her little sister's clinging arms. "It's our turn."

William had been only seven when his father had last seen him. He stared in shock at the tall fourteen-year-old lad facing him.

"Hello, Dad," William said, extending his hand and blushing scarlet to the roots of his hair.

"Hello, my big son," Father said and shook the hand. Then he pulled the gangling boy close before the blush had time to fade.

The first week was a wonderful and a taxing time. All the children felt it. The adults were equally on edge. Everybody tried not to be critical. Everybody tried not to show hurt feelings. But the young Gaulds felt as though they were walking a tightrope trying to please their actual parents and still show their deep love for the aunt and uncle who had stood in their place during the many years they had been absent.

It was a relief to all when the day for making the break neared. Father went ahead to Toronto to find them a house.

"I'm surprised you trust him that far, Gret," her sister said. "Men never look at what matters."

"What does matter?" Gretta asked, interested.

"The kitchen," both women said, speaking as one.

Then the family was back at the same station, only this time Gorrie was not being left behind. They got to know each other again during that train journey. None of the children let their mother see how much they already missed the Regina folk—not just their aunt and uncle but John and Dave and their friends.

Then they rolled into Union Station and Father, whom they were daring to call Dad now, was there to meet them. They had to have two taxi cabs to deliver them to the house William Gauld had found. Gorrie examined the kitchen with special attention and decided Dad had done very well indeed. There was a window above the sink and there was a gas stove which was hot instantly. The ice box was big too and it didn't leak. And there were lots of cupboards. She looked at her mother and understood her smile in a way she would not have done before hearing the women talking.

Harvey came home that night. Not knowing where to find his family, he went to Uncle George's house in Mimico. Seeing the place in darkness, he managed to force open the kitchen window, climbed through and fell into an exhausted sleep stretched out on the floor. His cousin Agnes, coming down to put the kettle on the next morning, saw him and, failing to recognize him after three years, went shrieking up the stairs to rouse her family.

What a funny story it made! How Agnes was teased!

Gorrie, looking up at him, understood Agnes's not knowing him. He had changed from a school-boy to a grown man. He even had a scruffy beard which he shaved off once they had all had time to take note of it.

After he had been royally welcomed, he went to see about his studies. He was told he would need to begin again as a first-year medical student. He was aggrieved about it but, in his heart, knew the pro-fessors were right. He had forgotten almost every-thing he had learned so long ago.

Then Dad took Gorrie to talk to the registrar at the University of Toronto about her schooling. Gorrie had told them, a bit defensively, that she wanted to be a doctor. They were less aghast than she had expected. After all, Molly Macdonald, who was a cousin of Mother's, had become a doctor when hardly any woman thought of taking such a revolutionary step.

"We need doctors badly in Taiwan," Dad said, studying her thoughtfully.

Gorrie kept quiet. She had no plan to be a doctor in Taiwan but the possibility was such a distant one she need not worry about it yet. First she had to fin-ish the necessary high-school courses and see if she could get in to medical school.

The registrar and Dad were old friends. They sat gossiping, at first, about their men friends. Gorrie tried not to wriggle. She felt very young. Finally they got around to discussing her future.

"Flora only has her Junior Matric since she went to school in Regina," Father told his old friend. "What subjects should she take in Fifth Form to get into university?"

"Do you really want to be a doctor, young woman?" the registrar asked, ignoring her father for the moment.

Gorrie thought of saying she was not sure because that would be the truth. Then she met his challenging level gaze.

"I do," she said.

"Then enrol now and don't waste time in high school," he said. "This is the last year anybody can become a doctor in five years. If you wait until next fall, you will have to spend six years in Meds and you'll be two years older when you graduate."

"She has lots of time," Dad rumbled, sitting back and eyeing his small determined daughter. "She only turned sixteen in March."

"It's up to you, Miss Gauld," the man behind the desk said. "You must make the decision. *Velut arbor aevo.*"

She did not need to ask for a translation. It was the motto of the University of Toronto and she had heard her father singing the Latin words all her life. It meant something like, "As a tree matures into age." Well, she might be only a sapling...or an acorn, come to that. But she would mature.

Flora Gauld filled in her application while the two men hovered over her like anxious birds watching a fledgling make its first flight.

When they came home and told the family the news, everyone was astounded and then amused. Only Harvey was silent. Having just been told he would have to begin again after three years in the trenches, he realized at once that he and Gorrie would be in the same class. That meant that he, now twenty-three, was going to be in the same class as a sixteen-year-old.

"Hy, will it be all right?" Gorrie said, under cover of the family laughter.

He met her anxious eyes with his.

"We'll see, won't we?" he said. "But there's one thing you'll have to do if we're going to be in the same class."

"What?" she asked.

"You'll have to put your hair up. It's all very well for a high-school girl to go around with her hair down her back and tied with a big floppy bow. It would embarrass me, and should embarrass you, for you to go to medical school looking like a baby."

"I'll try," Gorrie said slowly. She didn't want to, not one bit. She hated fussing. Hairpins never stayed where she put them. But, if it mattered that much, she would try.

"You can share books," Dorothy piped up.

"No," Harvey and Gorrie said in one voice.

"Second-hand books won't set us back too much," Dad said with his quiet smile.

The summer flew past. People kept dropping in. Gorrie got tired of making "burnt leather" cakes only to see them gobbled up at one sitting.

The night before her first lecture, she sat at her third-floor bedroom window trying to convince herself that she was looking forward to the morning.

"Flora, Cousin Molly is here," her mother called from the foot of the stairs. "Come on down. She wants to see you."

"Coming," Gorrie called back, stopping only to tie a fresh bow in the long dark hair gathered at the back of her neck. Tomorrow would be time enough to screw it into a topknot.

As she ran down the stairs, two steps at a time, she wondered for the first time what had given her mother's cousin the notion to become a doctor— plus the nerve to go through with it. Father supported Gorrie, but she was sure Mother and Aunt Jen might have been more comfortable if she had chosen nursing instead. After all, Florence Nightingale had turned nursing into a respectable career for girls of good family. Another cousin of Mother's was a nurse and she, Gorrie, could have gone into nursing, as Gretta was doing.

She arrived in the kitchen all eagerness to greet this visitor. Cousin Molly kissed her and then held her at arm's length so that their eyes could meet.

"I'm proud of you, Flora," she said, "but it won't be easy. You do know that, don't you?"

Her young cousin nodded.

"How was it for you?" Gretta asked from behind the ironing board.

Gorrie glanced at what she was pressing and saw the white blouse with its high collar that Gorrie planned to wear on the first day. Trust Gretta to be looking after her still.

Molly sat down, accepted a cup of tea and began remembering.

"When we four girls walked into class, we stuck together to keep our courage up. As soon as the boys saw us, they'd start stamping their feet on the wood floor and chanting, 'She doesn't know... That her degree... Should be MRS... And not MD.' They made up rude verses to go with that chorus."

"Why didn't your professors stop them?" Gorrie's mother asked, putting down a plate of fresh gingerbread.

"The boys only did it in classes where they knew the teacher was against women in medicine. They were quite safe," Molly said drily. "Some even egged them on by turning their backs and busying themselves copying notes onto the blackboard."

"What did you do to them?" Gorrie demanded, feeling hot anger on behalf of the handful of dedicated girls who had faced such callous taunts. Could she have done it?

"What could we do?" her cousin asked quietly. "We did what would irk them most. We kept on coming to classes, studying hard and passing every quiz. After a while, they got tired of baiting us. Only one girl gave up and went running home to her mama. I don't think she had the brains to graduate anyway."

"Cousin Molly, was it worth it?" Gretta asked, eyeing her younger sister. "Wouldn't you do differently now? I want to be a nurse but Gorrie is more and more set on trying for her MD."

"I don't regret my decision," their cousin said. "I practised only a brief time before I married. My husband would not hear of my going on with my medical career then. But I used my knowledge often in my home and to help other women. I hope, Flora, that you will not give up practising the way I did. Even if you decide to stay home with your children, you should somehow keep studying so that you can go back to active practice later."

Gorrie laughed.

"I haven't a sweetheart yet," she said, "let alone a husband and young children. Maybe I'll be like that girl you mentioned and run home to Mama before I've written my first exam."

"Not likely," her father said from the doorway. "You have set your hand to the..."

He hesitated, knowing "plough" was not the word he wanted.

"The hypodermic syringe," his daughter said, "and I will not turn back."

Everyone laughed, even her father. Gorrie felt more confident than she had in days. She was lucky to have Cousin Molly to back her her up and set her an example. She would be one of the few to have such a model.

Later, she and Gretta talked briefly of the tragedy in Cousin Molly's life. Her only son, Kit, who had been wild and unstable, had slit his wrists one night. He had done it when his mother was in the house and a blizzard was raging outside. He had run into the room where she sat, with blood running from both his arms, shouted something at her about being "better off dead" and then run out into the blinding snowstorm. She had tried to call him back but she could not leave his sisters alone while she struggled to find him. Standing at the open door, she had been unable to see two feet in front of her. The wind had hurled the whirling flakes into her face and she had known it would be insane to try to get help. No other houses were visible. She had waited, praying he would return. He had not come. Early the next morning, his body had been found in a deep snowdrift only a hundred yards from his own front door. All his mother's skill as a doctor had failed to save him.

That had happened years before. Her daughters had grown up without drama. And Cousin Molly had a quiet dignity now which discouraged prying. When she and Gorrie's mother got together, however, a merrier side of her surfaced. Then the two of them would laugh and joke, telling tales on each other and making fun of their husbands and children.

"They're crazy as loons," Gretta said tolerantly.

She and Gorrie both marvelled at their exuberance. Both women had suffered so much. How could they still be so funny? When had the shadow of Kit's brief life stopped haunting his mother? How had their own mother stood being separated from her children and having to learn of Gordon's death by cable? When their turn came to face such sorrows, would the two of them have the faith and the spunk of these two, laughing now over the day that Mother had made cream puffs for the British Consul's wife and put in salt instead of sugar?

As thirteen young women walked into their first medical lecture the next morning, nobody stamped or jeered openly.

"Well, well," the professor said, "what a bevy of beauties, eh, gentlemen? If you fail to keep your minds on Anatomy, I suppose I must understand."

The words were not hostile. But the voice in which they were spoken was distinctly cool. The male students laughed and turned in their seats to watch the girls enter.

The only empty chairs were at the very front. As they trooped down the stairs of the lecture theatre, their sensible shoes sounded louder than a herd of iron-shod horses. Gorrie took out her notebook and tried hard to look older than sixteen.

She also forced herself not to look around for her brother Harvey. She knew he would be uncomfortable if the relationship were discovered too early. The terrible sights he had had to witness in the trenches had turned him into a man but had left her still a child in his eyes.

Well, she had put her hair up to please him. She carried her head carefully upright, dreading the moment the edifice came undone. Sooner or later, she was convinced, her tresses would come tumbling down as surely as the walls of Jericho.

Except for the fact that she seemed to break retorts and test tubes every single time she had to work in the chemistry lab, Flora Gauld found she was as good a medical student as anyone else, the boys included.

Then, one November day, she took home a bag of human bones to study. When she came in with them, her father smiled at her.

"What have you there?" he asked, eyeing the brown paper bag.

Gorrie claimed later that she had intended to say "bones" but the word "buns" slipped out accidentally. She herself was not certain whether or not she spoke the truth.

"Just what I need," her father said and reached into the bag.

When his fingers closed on a tibia, he could not believe it. He snatched his hand out of the bag as though he had been burned. Then he preached her an extemporaneous sermon on the sanctity of human remains.

"Think, daughter, that each of those dry bones was once part of a living person," he lectured her. "How can you be so unfeeling as to treat them with such flippancy? I cannot believe you are really so callous."

Gorrie opened her mouth to tell him of the irreverence with which medical students viewed cadavers, of the human skulls she had seen being used as

ashtrays and paperweights, of the ribald jokes her
fellows made about various body parts. It was the
only way they could keep doing some of the grisly
tasks required of them. If she had not hardened herself to such things, she would have been forced to
quit long before this.

Then she looked into her father's troubled face
and held her peace. It was the first time in her life
that she had felt years older than one of her parents.

That night, Mother called her down to the
kitchen for a talk. Gorrie was sure she was going to
be scolded for not studying but she was wrong.

"Your father and I are both so worried about
Harvey," she said, holding Gorrie's hand in hers.
"He isn't working the way he should."

Gorrie knew. Her bedroom was next to her
brother's, and she heard him pacing the floor. He
was missing Gordon, she knew, and he was thinking about those things he had once described to her.
He was also head over heels in love with Marjorie
White, the girl Gordon had wanted to marry. How
could they expect him to pore over his Anatomy
text?

"It's hard for Hy," she said, not meeting her
mother's eyes. "Probably he just needs time."

"Your father and I want you to try talking to
him," Mother said.

Gorrie snatched her hand away.

"Me?" she said, horrified at the very thought.
"Why me? I couldn't."

"You are taking the same courses." Mother

recaptured her hand and gripped it tightly. "He'd listen to you, Flora. If anyone can do it, you can. He thinks the sun rises and sets on you."

"Ask Marjorie. He'd do anything for her," Gorrie muttered, beginning to feel trapped.

"Marjorie doesn't love him. She was going to marry Gordon. She's being kind to Harvey for his brother's sake but seeing him makes her grief harder to bear. We can't ask more of her. Flora, watch for a chance and just try."

Gorrie bolted up the stairs, escaping from her mother's pleading gaze with relief. But she knew she would have to do what they had asked of her, even if Hy would never speak to her again.

She coaxed him out for a walk the next night and did her best. She heard herself sounding timid and priggish and plaintive. She was not surprised when he swore at her and told her to mind her own business.

He did not speak to her for two days.

Her parents, guessing at what had happened to start this coldness, waited guiltily.

Then he came to her door with a bag of maple sugar candies he had bought.

"Peace offering," he said, with his old grin. "But never lecture me again, youngster. Not if you value your life."

"I won't, Hy. I promise," she said, her eyes filling with sudden unwelcome tears.

"Turn off the waterworks," he jibed. "I haven't time to wipe your nose. I have to study for the

Anatomy test tomorrow. I'm being a good little boy tonight."

As he turned to go back to his own room, she measured his towering six-foot-tall body with her eyes. He was not a little boy. She would never presume to interfere with his life again.

Dorothy had left a book on Gorrie's bed earlier. She abandoned her own studies and picked it up. She deserved a treat after the last couple of days. It was a copy of *Little Women*. She felt akin to Jo March in a new way. As the March family read *Pilgrim's Progress* and struggled to be like Christian facing his many temptations, and as Jo found herself not fitting in to the role of prim and proper young miss, so she, Gorrie Gauld, had to fight to be the daughter her parents expected. It was hard. Then she came to the part when Mr. Laurence asked Jo to talk to Laurie about his studies. The outcome was the same as her efforts with Harvey. She laughed out loud and read on.

"How's the Anatomy coming?" a teasing voice inquired.

"Go away, brother," Gorrie threatened, "or I'll throw the book at you."

She finished it at one in the morning. Getting into her nightgown, she laughed softly. She was the one who was going to flunk the test. Would Hy be asked to talk to her next?

"Just let him try," she murmured and turned out the light.

12
A Kindred Spirit

In the bleak midwinter,
Frosty wind made moan.
Earth was hard as iron,
Water like a stone.
Snow had fallen, snow on snow,
Snow on snow,
In the bleak midwinter,
Long ago.
 Christina Rossetti

"Flora, would you wait a minute?" Mary Ann Banks said as her Sunday School class got ready to go.

"Of course," Gorrie said. She sat down again, still holding her Bible and her copy of *The Youth's Companion*. She hoped Miss Banks had time to spare. She needed someone to talk to these days.

"How are things going at home?" her teacher asked gently, as though reading Gorrie's thoughts.

Gorrie did not know where to begin.

"Your parents?" the teacher prompted. "They must be nearly over the shock of finding you all grown up? It can't have been easy."

"It hasn't been easy for any of us," Gorrie blurted out. "We've never all lived together before. When they left, I was just nine. Dad's so different from Uncle Jack. And Mother's like Aunt Jen in some ways but she isn't in others. I miss Aunt Jen so much but I can't say so because it hurts Mother. And they are still grieving for Gordon."

"How's Harvey getting along? Gordon's death must have been a great shock to him," Mary Ann Banks said.

"Harvey and I are the only two on the third floor," Gorrie told her. "At night, I hear him pacing back and forth, back and forth. He must be thinking of his time in the trenches. He seems so changed. Haunted, I guess. But he doesn't talk to anyone about it. Having me in his class hasn't helped."

She did not say she was afraid that sometime he might break down and pour it all out to her. She didn't think she could bear it. And she knew she was not wise enough to help him. Gretta and she had talked about it once and they had agreed that he must feel he should have died in Gordon's place. After all, Gord was their parents' firstborn and he had always seemed the most gifted.

She and her teacher were silent for a long moment. Then Gorrie added, in a low voice, "I want them all to be happy. We've yearned to be together as a family for so long. Even without

Gordon, it should be like a dream come true. Yet their furlough is half over. I feel as though we're letting it go to waste."

Mary Ann Banks looked into Gorrie's worried eyes.

"Dreams are often too big and grand ever to be wholly real," she said gently. "Perhaps you could help make it a bit more true by taking on one piece of it at a time. You might devote an hour to Gretta, for instance. You'll work it out. I also have a favour to ask."

Gorrie, her thoughts on her family, was only half-listening. Her teacher waited.

"Of course," Gorrie said, the moment she took in the silence. "If I can help..."

"Before you came to Toronto, I got to know a girl a little older than you who needed a friend badly. Her name is Ida Raymond and she has a tubercular hip so she can't come to church. On Sunday afternoon, I take her the Sunday School papers. She lives with a cousin who is not a reader and can't understand Ida's need for almost any reading matter. I can't go today and they have no telephone. You go right past her place on your way home. Would you mind dropping in and telling her how sorry I am to miss our visit?"

"I'd be glad to go," Gorrie said, feeling shy at the thought.

"Good. I think the two of you are kindred spirits. Ida badly needs a friend closer to her own age."

Gorrie rose. Mary Ann's earlier words had given

her an idea for a way to help her family. She was eager to begin trying it. But she was curious about this Miss Ida Raymond too.

It was a freezing February day. As she hurried down the icy street, Gorrie looked up at the row of grey buildings jammed one against the next. On the ground level were crowded, shabby stores, and above them were apartment windows looking down on the noisy street. Here and there, net curtains hung limply or a lonely flowerpot showed somebody's attempt to give even bleak poverty a touch of warmth. It made the cold even colder.

She could not imagine living up there as this Miss Raymond did. How did they get enough clean air to breathe? Then she arrived at the address she had been given.

Despite the bitter weather, the street door leading to a dark staircase was open a crack. Gorrie hesitated. It looked dingy and uninviting and a smell of stale boiled cabbage oozed through it—boiled cabbage and unwashed human beings. Gorrie soon discovered why the door had not been closed in spite of the bone-chilling cold. It was stuck that way. At last she swallowed hard and, squeezing through the gap, started to climb the narrow, steep stairs that mounted to the fourth floor. There had been a railing once but most of it was long gone.

Up and up she went, passing one landing with a closed door behind which a fretful baby wailed and another where there was no sound at all. No warmth came out from under the doors. Then she was labouring up the final flight. Even though she often ran up the stairs at home without becoming breathless, she found herself gasping now. Having no bannister was only a small part of it. The extreme cold and the sickening stench made her feel as though there was a lack of oxygen.

"Her cousin often leaves her alone. She can't come to the door easily even on her best days," Miss Banks had said. "So just go on in once she answers."

Gorrie thought of Red Riding Hood's mother telling her to "knock on the door, lift the latch and walk in." Wasn't it dangerous leaving a sick girl by herself behind an unlocked door? Weren't there wolves in Toronto? Or did she imagine that because she was from Regina where almost everybody knew almost everybody else?

She stood stock-still in front of the door, longing to turn and run.

Baby, she jeered at herself and lifted her hand and knocked lightly.

"Come in," called a tired voice.

Gorrie turned the knob and pushed open the door. Across from her on a couch, a pale girl bundled in a thin blanket and knitted shawl lay watching her.

"Hello, Miss Raymond," Gorrie panted. "Miss Banks sent me."

She got no further. The girl propped herself up on her elbow and smiled. Her thin face was transformed by that smile.

"Oh, she never forgets," she said. "And I think you must be Flora Gauld. She's told me about you and she promised to see that I met you one day."

Gorrie felt her own shyness begin to melt away. But she was anxious about Ida, who had now dropped back onto her pillows. Her face was so gaunt and wasted that her dark eyes looked enormous. And Gorrie could tell that she had spent many hours in pain. Now, because she had raised herself that way to greet her visitor, her forehead was beaded with sweat and her hands trembled.

Gorrie put down the Sunday School papers. Then she pulled up a rickety chair and seated herself. She did not take her coat off but she removed her gloves and scarf. She did not know where to start talking with Ida so, to give both of them a moment's respite, she glanced around the room.

Her own family had no money to spend on luxuries but their home was a palace compared with this. The couch on which the other girl lay was lumpy and the fabric covering it was threadbare. It looked far from comfortable. The cushions supporting her were bunched up awkwardly. Gorrie made up her mind then and there to rearrange them before she left.

One small poinsettia in a pot gave the room its only spot of colour. But the plant was drooping for lack of water. There was another spindly chair like the one she sat on and one other upholstered one. It looked a little more comfortable than the old couch but not much. A door to her left opened into a bedroom which also held a minimum of furniture. One corner was curtained off. A commode chair could be glimpsed where the curtain was not quite closed.

"I'm sorry Betty is out," Ida said. "If she were here, I'd get her to make you some tea."

"Could I make it?" Gorrie said. "Or, if that's not possible, I'd love a glass of water. And perhaps I can give the poinsettia a drink while I'm at it."

Ida Raymond looked down at the floor for a moment and made no answer. Then she raised her head and looked straight at her guest.

"That would be lovely except for the fact that the pump is away down on the ground floor just inside the door," she said grimly. "Betty has to carry our water up in that bucket. She meant to fetch some before she left but she was late."

Without a word, Gorrie rose, picked up the pail and went swiftly down to the pump. She had to wait while a stout woman in a dressing gown and slippers got some first.

"At least it's working today," the woman said stoically. "Sometimes it freezes up and we have to go next door."

Gorrie put her rage into the pumping when her turn came. Water spurted into her bucket. The woman turned and gave her a weary smile.

"I used to go at it like that," she said, "before I had the baby. Now I'm too tired and too scared the bloody thing will break."

Gorrie swung the pump handle a little more gently, but not much. When the pail was full, she lugged it up to the Raymonds' rooms. Long before she got there, she felt some sympathy for Ida's cousin. It wasn't easy getting a full bucket up the interminable flight of steps.

As she tramped in through the open door, the pail knocked against the door jamb and some of the precious water slopped out and soaked her right shoe. At her smothered "Damn!" Ida Raymond laughed. The sound was sweet.

"You should see your face," she said. "It *is* pretty bad, isn't it? When my parents were alive, I had a proper home. We were poor, you know, but we had a small house with two shade trees and we actually had a pump in the kitchen. It always gave us lots of cold well water. But they died of typhoid fever when I was eleven and Betty had to take me in. It hasn't been easy for either of us. She could not live with the disgrace of having her cousin in the poorhouse but she isn't cut out to nurse a semi-invalid."

Gorrie had never seen inside a poorhouse but she thought Ida might have fared better there or in a hospital than here. She found a tumbler and a cup. Using the dipper that hung above the pail, she gave herself and Ida a drink. Then she took some across to the poinsettia. "A lady from the church sent me the flower," Ida said. "I love it but it's hard to have to share our water with a plant."

Gorrie nodded. Before she sat down again, she hoisted Ida up and punched the pillows into a more comfortable position.

"Are you alone a lot?" she asked.

Ida laughed again, but there was a bitter note to the laughter.

"Betty likes gossiping with the neighbours better than sitting with me," she said. "She talks all the time so I find it more restful without her. She loves to play cards too. I'm not good at it."

"Would you like me to read you the *Companion*?" Gorrie asked, putting her gloves back on before her hands froze. Her toes inside the wet shoe were slowly turning into blocks of ice.

Ida glanced at the magazine.

"I would," she said, "but I'd rather talk, if you don't mind. Miss Banks has told me all about you and your family. What a life you have had! And you are in medical school. Are you really just sixteen?"

Gorrie nodded.

"I'll be seventeen in March," she admitted. "I'm the youngest one there. I wouldn't admit this to my family but looking ahead scares me silly."

"I'd be terrified," Ida said, "and I'm nearly twenty."

They were off then, each interested in the other, each needing a sympathetic ear.

"How many of you Gaulds are there?" Ida asked.

"Mother and Dad came home from Formosa in January," Gorrie said. "Harvey, my older brother, came home from the trenches during the winter. My sister Gretta has started training to be a nurse at Sick Children's Hospital and William is in high school now. My little sister, Dorothy, is with us too. She's eleven."

"Mary Ann told me about your other brother being killed overseas," Ida said. "I haven't had to face any heartbreak like that."

Gorrie looked into the other girl's face and saw she was perfectly sincere. Even though her life had been so much harder than Gorrie's, she felt Flora Gauld had suffered more than she.

"Gordon was ten years older than I," Gorrie said slowly, looking down at her gloved fingers, "and he was away from me mostly, first at school and then in the war. I knew him and I loved him. We all looked up to him. Yet now he seems unreal to me. Not a stranger and yet not close like William, who's just a year younger than I. My parents miss him dreadfully, of course, and so does Harvey. But I feel strange knowing they miss him so much more than I do. I haven't told this to anyone else."

"It must be wonderful though to have such a large, close family to share the hurt with," Ida said. "When my parents died, Betty was more or less a stranger. She had to take care of me and that worried her. She didn't miss them because she scarcely knew them. It was a queer, nightmare time. It seems long ago now but I still remember yearning for one person to understand how alone I felt."

Then both girls heard someone coming up the stairs. Ida listened. Her face took on a look of resignation.

"It's Betty," she said. "But promise, before she

gets here, that you'll come back."

Gorrie nodded. She could hear Betty's feet slowing as she started up the last flight. The minute she came through the door, the atmosphere was radically altered.

"Well, well, we have company, I see," she said. Not waiting for Ida to introduce her guest or explain what she was doing there, Betty went over to a small gas heater in the corner and lit it. She stood over it, warming her hands as the flame strengthened. She talked all through this, as though she saw nothing amiss in leaving her cousin in an unheated room. "How lucky you are, Ida Raymond, lying down at your ease while other people have to go out in that biting wind! I'm worn out. You aren't starving, are you? I don't see how you could get hungry moving around so little. Mrs. Gowdie insisted I have a sandwich with her before she would let me go. It was the least she could do since she won every game we played practically. Oh, are you going, dear?"

"She is," Ida said flatly, "but she's coming again. Her name is Flora Gauld, if you're interested."

"Of course I'm interested," Betty said huffily. Then she spotted the bucket of water still half full.

"Oh, heavens, you've drunk up almost all the water," she complained, as though she'd filled the pail to the brim before she departed.

Gorrie's mouth opened and shut. Ida, watching her, smothered a giggle. Her cousin dipped out enough water to fill the kettle for tea, splashing it in as though they had plenty more. Then, having near-ly emptied the pail, she smiled a wide sugary smile at Gorrie.

"You're so young and strong, dear," she said, holding out the bucket and fluttering her eyelashes, "Would you mind very much…?"

"No, Betty," Ida said.

Gorrie, who had risen to go, halted. She was angry at the selfish woman for trying to work on her sympathies so crassly. But she had a feeling that Ida might not get a second cup if Betty had to fetch more water. She reached for the handle, dumped what water remained into the dipper on the table, and turned to go out the door without speaking a word.

"Miss Gauld, you needn't," Ida said, her thin cheeks reddening with embarrassment.

"I don't mind," Gorrie told her gently, not look-ing at the older woman, who was back at the gas heater.

"You shouldn't have asked her, Betty," Gorrie heard Ida say furiously as she started down the stairs. "She got the last bucket, as you very well know."

"She said she doesn't mind," the woman whined. "I had palpitations on the second landing."

Gorrie grinned and went running on down the stairs lickety-split. She wanted to race back up and be done with the whole business but she couldn't do it without spilling the water. Before she reached the Raymonds' door, she could hear Betty's petu-lant voice.

"It's not my fault, Ida, that I'm over forty and my legs aren't what they used to be. If I had the money, I'd move down to a ground floor flat, as you know, but whatever anyone says, it costs more to feed two than one…"

Feeling sickened by her insensitivity, Gorrie marched in and put down the pail of water.

"I must go. My family will be wondering where I've gone," she said. "But your cousin hasn't had a bite to eat. I'm sure she'd feel better with something in her stomach. I'll be back, Miss Raymond, I promise."

Ida's look of gratitude comforted her a little as she plunged down the stairs again and out to the street. All the way home, she felt the wind cutting through her wool coat and ached for Ida, half frozen and yet so gallant. Even a first-year medical student knew it must be bad for Ida to huddle hour after hour in that ice-box of a room. The stifling heat of summer would be even worse, she was certain. Ida should be in the mountains somewhere, where she would have at least a chance of getting better. Instead, Gorrie knew, she was going to die up there.

"I can't stand her dying," Gorrie whispered. "I shouldn't be a doctor. I'll be no good at it."

Home seemed like heaven to her that afternoon. She felt guilty when she turned on the kitchen tap and piping hot water gushed out of the spigot. She washed her hands and then ran a glass of cold water to drink. She drained the last precious drop, filled the glass again and made up her mind to take Ida some fresh fruit next time she went. Maybe some juicy oranges or a melon would somehow make up to her a little. In her room, she took out the diary her father had given her.

"Today is Gretta's day," she wrote. "She's a brick. She shall have tomorrow too."

No matter how much her sister annoyed her at times, she knew, after only fifteen minutes with Ida's awful cousin, how deeply she loved her. She loved them all. And they loved her back.

Tomorrow she would get home in time to make them one of her burnt leather cakes. A big one. William always wanted three pieces.

13
The Watch That Ends the Night

Abide with me: fast falls the eventide,
The darkness deepens: Lord, with me abide:
When other helpers fail, and comforts flee,
Help of the helpless, O abide with me.
Henry Francis Lyte

As winter turned to spring, Gorrie's studies required more of her time and she neglected her new friend. But once she had finished her final exam, she returned to the tenement.

"Oh, Flora...Miss Gauld, I mean," Ida cried with delight, the moment Gorrie came puffing into view.

"Call me Gorrie. I've called you Ida inside my head for ages," Gorrie said, wiping away the sweat that was running down her face.

The two bleak rooms Ida shared with Betty were certainly no longer cold. They had become ovens instead. Carrying up water to the lonely young woman became terribly important. But no matter what she did, Gorrie saw Ida growing more ill. One especially sweltering day in June, she bought an ice-cream cone from a street vendor and ran all the way up the four flights to thrust it into Ida's hand. It was running down Ida's wrist before she could manage more than a couple of licks but it was worth the effort just to see her laugh.

One afternoon, she reached the tenement to find Ida sitting just outside the street door on a chair. She looked absolutely exhausted but she smiled radiantly when she saw Gorrie.

"I felt better so I made up my mind to come down here," she said.

"How did you ever do it?"

"Step by step, on my seat," Ida bragged. But she had to breathe in between words. And, to Gorrie's anxious eyes, she looked much more frail than when she had first seen her.

"I think you've had enough perhaps," she said gently.

Ida gave a ghost of a laugh.

"I think you're right," she said. "But I don't see how I'm going to make it."

Gorrie looked around. A couple of husky boys were kicking a battered ball about in the vacant lot across the street. She called to them. When she explained what she wanted, they grinned at her.

"Sure," said the taller one.

Ida protested only faintly as they made a seat with their linked hands and Gorrie helped her onto it. At the first landing, Gorrie was sure none of them would make it. She supported Ida while the boys caught their breath. Then on they all went.

At last they were at the Raymonds' door. Gorrie had brought Ida some apples. She gave them to the boys instead. Then the two of them went galloping down the stairs at breakneck speed.

"I can't even imagine running now," her friend said wearily. "Could you help me to bed?"

It was mid-afternoon but Gorrie made no protest. As she helped Ida into her cheap cotton nightgown, she knew, all at once, that her friend would never leave the little apartment again.

That night, she almost told her parents she had changed her mind about becoming a doctor. She could teach instead. Gretta had taught when she was seventeen. But something held Gorrie back from saying anything.

The following Sunday, Mary Ann Banks told her that the doctor felt Ida had only a few days left to live.

"I was there last night," she said quietly, "and she asked to see you, Flora. Do you think...?"

Gorrie was afraid. She knew, with shame, that it was fear, not busyness, that had kept her from visiting Ida for the past ten days.

"I'll go tonight," she said.

When she got there, Betty and three other women were playing euchre in the main room. Ida's cousin gave Gorrie a guilty look.

"She's better tonight or I wouldn't be out here,

as you can imagine," she gabbled. "She was half-asleep last time I peeped in. I asked if she just wanted to be alone to rest and she said 'Yes.' I'm sure she'd like to see you though."

Despite the words, Gorrie saw her own fear reflected back at her in Betty's eyes.

"I'll sit with her," she said more gently than she usually spoke to Betty. "You go on with your game."

When she reached Ida's bedside, she thought, for one heartstopping moment, that her friend had already died. Then Ida drew in a rasping breath that shook her wasted body. Gorrie pulled the only chair in the room close to the bedside and took the transparently thin hand in both of hers. Fiercely she willed herself not to cry.

Ida did not seem to know Gorrie was there at first. Then her eyelids fluttered open.

"I'm...glad...it's...you," she whispered. "I'm so cold."

Gorrie felt the stifling heat in the tiny room pressing down upon her. She moved to the bed and, not needing to think about what to do, gathered Ida's pitifully thin body into her arms, resting the dying girl's head against her own shoulder.

"It is cold," she lied, "but I'm still hot. Perhaps I can warm you up."

Ida made no answer. She nestled into Gorrie's strong arms with a long sigh like a lost child who has, at last, found her mother. Neither of them spoke. Gorrie rocked slowly back and forth, back and forth. She found herself beginning to sing "Abide with Me" and stopped.

"Go on," she heard Ida whisper.

"Abide with me. Fast falls the eventide," Gorrie sang huskily. "The darkness deepens…"

She stopped. Ida stirred against her.

"I can't go on," Gorrie whispered.

Next door, the four women laughed. Gorrie had to will herself not to stiffen. They did not know what was happening in the dark bedroom. The doctor must have told Betty that Ida's life would soon end but Betty either had not understood or had simply refused to believe he spoke the truth. Gorrie hoped the woman would not come in, not yet.

She was holding one of Ida's hands. She felt the fingertips grow chill. Ida was slipping into a coma. Then she roused and murmured words Gorrie had to strain to catch.

"The water is so deep."

Gorrie went on rocking. She still could not sing. Ida's hand was icy now. Then the whispered words came again, more laboured, fainter.

"It's dark and the water is so deep. I…"

No more words. Gorrie had been with dying people before but never alone. Never with a friend who was still so young. Should she get Betty? Was Ida fighting her way back because she wanted to say goodbye to the woman who had taken her in but never understood or truly loved her?

"Shall I get Betty?" she asked, her voice almost as soft as Ida's.

The head against her shoulder shook ever so slightly. Time passed. Then Ida spoke once more.

"She'll be…so…alone. I wish…"

Gorrie took a deep breath. She knew before she spoke that Betty would not welcome any comfort she might try to give. But she had to set Ida free, if she could.

"I'll be her friend, Ida," she said in a clear, steady voice. "If she wants me to, I'll be her friend."

Ida sighed. Then she spoke for the last time.

"Sing while I…go."

Gorrie tried. She began at the beginning again.

> "Abide with me. Fast falls the even-
> tide. The darkness deepens. Lord, with
> me abide…"

This time, while Gorrie sang, Ida went out into the darkness and did not return.

When the shallow, uneven breathing ceased, the room was suddenly still. The girl left alive felt swallowed up and small in the immense silence. She waited a few seconds longer, hardly breathing herself. Then she laid the lifeless body down, kissed the cool cheek and stumbled toward the door.

As she opened it, one of the women said, "Betty, I can't believe you can be so lucky."

Betty did not answer. She had caught sight of Gorrie's face, now streaming with tears.

"Oh, my God, no," she cried and knocked her chair over, rushing into the bedroom.

Twenty minutes later, Gorrie was out on the street running for home. Ida no longer needed her. Betty not only did not need her, she was angry at her for not having called her sooner. Gorrie had longed to say that Ida had not wanted her to but, with a great effort of will, she had held her tongue.

She knew, if Ida did not, that Betty Raymond disliked her. They would never be friends. They were far too different. And Betty could not forgive a seventeen-year-old for somehow meaning more to her cousin than she did.

When Gorrie reached home, she ran up the steps and into her father's arms. He held her as tenderly as she had held Ida an hour before. She could not stop crying for a long time.

"Flora, perhaps you should think again about becoming a doctor," he said after she had, haltingly, told him about Ida's death. "It may be too much for you."

Gorrie raised her head and stared at his serious, kind face in blank astonishment.

She had thought the same thing a week ago. But somehow everything was different, changed by what she had just been through.

"I'm too tired to think now," she gulped. "Will you call Miss Banks and tell her?"

When Gorrie wakened late the following morning, she found that her mother and Mary Ann Banks had packed a suitcase for her.

"I'm taking you to Muskoka," her teacher said.

"You need a holiday before you begin your second year. Don't argue. Betty doesn't want us at the funeral. The kindest thing we can do for her, right now, is leave town."

They took a train and then a boat. Gorrie went along in a daze. She knew she must think but something stopped her from even trying.

Three days later, at sunset, she sat alone on a bluff looking down on Lake Rosseau. The wind ruffled the water so that its sunset gold kept spilling into new lines and then smoothing out into a satiny sheen again. Bats were wheeling above her. The last sleepy birds called good-night to each other. A loon laughed. Gorrie sat very still, drinking in the beauty, letting it ease her pain.

She knew then, without needing to talk it over with anyone, that she would go on to be a doctor no matter how hard it was. There would be other Idas who needed a friend. And needed other things too. Cool water when they were burning up. Someone to hold onto. Gorrie was only seventeen and she was still afraid, but she had been tested. She could do it.

It was like marching through a dark wood, singing "Dare to be a Daniel" at the top of your voice, and suddenly finding yourself in the open again.

Gorrie smiled and sang softly to Ida and to the sunset and to the stars which were beginning to light the darkening sky.

Day is done.
Gone the sun
From the lake,
   from the hills,
         from the sky.
All is well.
Safely rest.
God is nigh.

Epilogue

◈

What happened after that?

In September 1921, Gorrie Gauld went to a meeting of the Student Christian Movement. At nineteen, she was in her final year of Meds. Looking around, she noticed a new face.

"Who's he, Vic?" she asked Victoria Chung.

"Llew Little. He's just started even though he's older. But then everyone's older than you, Gorrie," her friend teased.

Laughing, Gorrie forgot the new man. As the night wore on though, she kept noticing him. He was such a funny mixture, joking wickedly one minute and deeply serious the next. She liked him.

After that, her ears pricked up at the sound of his name. He was twenty-three! She found herself wondering about his background and his dreams. He was wondering too. Her name kept cropping up in his diary. At Christmas, he wrote:

Gorrie G! I have never met a girl with
such native charm, intuitive good
sense, sound philosophy of life,
divinely human in her ways, and
one who is so well qualified for her
Master's work.

They grew close. He told her of his family in
Guelph. His father, a stonemason, had been killed
in an accident when Llew was just fourteen. He had
quit school and worked in a butcher shop to help
his mother make ends meet. Then a friend had persuaded him to attend night classes. Now a high
school graduate, he was working his way through
college.

"I still try to send money home but it's hard," he
said. Without my sister Eva's office job, we couldn't
manage. She's a brick."

Gorrie admired him but, once in a while, he
seemed too high-minded and stuffy. One night, he
phoned to ask if she'd like to go for a walk. Not in
the mood to listen to him talk on and on about himself, she said she was sorry but she had to study. An
hour later, a friend of Llew's called to invite her to a
hockey game. She went like a shot. Llew found out,
of course, and his ardour cooled. She, with a philo-
sophical shrug, wrote in her diary:

"Oh, well, that's that, I suppose. Too
bad."

His hurt was short-lived. His diary soon read:

> Gorrie G! Not one whit of a disappoint-
> ment. The finest in 10,000 X 10. A
> healthy mind, a high soul, a hopeful
> outlook and a kind friend.

Early in May, 1923, when she was an intern at Women's College Hospital and he was finishing his second year in Meds, he took her to a restaurant and proposed.

"I have a story to tell you," he said. "There was once a poor boy who loved a princess. He longed to marry her but he knew he was unworthy. He took her to a restaurant where, if she was not interested, she could simply dunk him lightly in the lemonade, and they could still be friends."

He waited. She sipped lemonade and tried to think what to say. She was about to graduate; he had four years to go. Both had debts. She hadn't enough to pay the fee required to change her M.B. into an M.D. Neither had enough money to marry. His mother still depended on his financial help.

"I love you, Llew," she said at last, "but we can't marry for years. I need to think. Give me time."

"Of course," he said. But, knowing she loved him, he returned home walking on air.

In June, they went canoeing on the Humber river. She waited until they were in deep water before she said "Yes." He almost overturned the canoe.

They had four years to wait. She planned to

become a resident at a mental hospital where she would be paid enough to clear her debts. Then Margaret Ann Gauld wrote from Taiwan. The doctor there badly needed to go on furlough. If her mother paid her passage, would Flora consider taking his place temporarily?

Gretta was already there. In spite of her determination never to follow in her parents' footsteps, Gorrie's big sister was to spend over forty years as a missionary nurse in Taiwan.

Formosa was a long way away from Llew. But Gorrie was needed both by the hospital and by her recently widowed mother and older sister. With mixed feelings, Flora Gauld packed her bags. Although Llew did visit her once in Taiwan, she did not return to Canada for four years.

In 1927, on her way home to be married, Gorrie stopped in Regina to see the Balfours and stayed two extra days. Yet, when the train pulled into Union Station, Llew was there, grinning from ear to ear.

"How did you know I'd be on this train?" she marvelled, giving him a quick kiss.

"I didn't," he said. "I've met all the trains from the west for three days."

She wrote in her diary that night:

> "Llew is not only as dear as ever
> but infinitely dearer."

In order to talk undisturbed, the two of them took a streetcar ride. During it, they decided to be married that very afternoon if he could get a special license. His mother was unwell and they did not want her to be faced with putting on a grand wedding for her dear Llew.

"She'll cry a bit and scold us," Gorrie said, "but in her heart, she'll be vastly relieved."

She did not admit that she, Gorrie Gauld, always uncomfortable in the limelight, would be relieved too.

They got the special license. Gorrie phoned her sister Dorothy, who had come home with her, and Llew called his best friend.

"If you want to see us married, be at Bloor St. Church at three," they told them.

Her wedding dress was a suit she'd had for five years. There was no bouquet, no bridesmaid, no fancy wedding cake. But the love they had for each other that day was so deep that it lasted the rest of their lives.

In Guelph, his family had been expecting the pair to arrive for two days. His fourteen-year-old sister Ruth cooked a chicken dinner in celebration of Gorrie's homecoming. When the young couple did not arrive, Llew's mother and sisters were disappointed but Ruth said she'd cook another. When the couple failed to arrive on the second evening though, Ruth was fed up.

"If they come tomorrow," she declared, "they're having pork and beans. And they'll like it or lump it."

Llew and Flora Little, newly married, walked

through the door and, amid teasing and tears, sat down to a banquet of pork and beans. They liked them so much that they had them on every anniversary.

They worked together in the small town of Matheson in northern Ontario. Their first child Jamie was born there. Flora was contented but Llew was restless. So they went to Toronto for more study. Then, without much urging, they sailed for Taiwan where their medical skill was needed. In the next ten years, they had three more children, Jean, Hugh and Patricia.

I told the stories of my life as Gorrie's daughter in my books *Little By Little* and *Stars Come Out Within*.

Flora Gauld Little died at her home on July 11, 1991 after a long battle with bone cancer. We, her children, were all with her when her life ended. Her epitaph reads

Flora Gauld Little M.B.

1902 – 1991

HER LIGHT STILL SHINES

Acknowledgments

◈

Many people have helped me make this book as historically accurate as possible. My inability to read print made the checking of facts extremely difficult. I am well aware that there are inaccuracies I have missed. I would have slipped up even more often without the help of the following people.

Sally MacCrae and Rupert Evans found out where the train stopped in 1907, Jenny Stephens asked members of her congregations the names of horse-drawn carriages used by families in 1907 and located not only the words to all the old hymns I wanted to use but the names of their authors and the probable dates of their composition; May Lee Richardson and Kim Bhun Chung helped me with the spellings of Chinese names and told me not to worry too much because there were no absolutely right answers; Lynn Carr looked up the name of the park in Regina which Gorrie skipped through on her way to the dentist's office and gave me the date of the cyclone; George Hindley looked up the information about the sinking of the *Lusitania* and translated "Velut Arbor Aevo" for me; Ruth Workman, the author of *Kippen and Its Families* (Seaforth 1982), provided me with a rich fund of stories, one of which I moved ahead several years so that Gorrie could be in on it; Carlotta Hacker, the author of *The Indomitable Lady Doctors* told me when Cousin Molly graduated and how many women were in Gorrie's class; Mary Rubio kept me from having Gorrie read a book that had not yet been published.

Thank you.

If I mentioned everyone who helped, the Acknowledgments would be longer than the novel. If anyone knows the source of something I have overlooked, please write me so that I can include it in future editions.

None of the people named above is responsible, however, for the use or misuse I made of the facts I was given. My hope is that my readers will be too taken up with Gorrie's story to care.

Jean Little